DAVID'S DAUGHTER, TAMAR

MARGARET BARRINGTON was born on 10 May 1896 at Malin, County Donegal. Her father was a District Inspector of Police in the R.I.C. She attended a girls grammar school in Dungannon, a convent school in Valentia, Co. Kerry, Alexandra College in Dublin and a French school in Normandy before going to Trinity College, Dublin in 1915. She married historian Edmund Curtis in 1922. The marriage was dissolved and, in 1926 she married Liam O'Flaherty. They travelled widely in Ireland, England and France before separating in 1932. During the 1930s she lived in England, publishing her novel *My Cousin Justine* (Cape/Random House) writing short stories and contributing a women's page to the *Tribune*. She was also politically active, helping refugees from Nazi Germany and organising support for the Republican side in the Spanish Civil War. When the Second World War broke out, she moved to West Cork, continuing to write short stories and articles.

Margaret Barrington died on 8th March 1982.

DAVID'S DAUGHTER, TAMAR

MARGARET BARRINGTON

Introduced by William Trevor

Wolfhound Press

482025025

01860975

© 1982 Margaret Barrington

First published in 1982 by
WOLFHOUND PRESS
68 Mountjoy Square, Dublin 1.

British Library Cataloguing in Publication Data
    Barrington, Margaret
        David's daughter, Tamar.
        I. Title
        823'.914 [F]   PR6052.A/

        ISBN 0-905473-87-6
        ISBN 0-905473-74-4 Pbk

This book is published with the assistance of
The Arts Council (An Chomhairle Ealaíon), Dublin, Ireland.

CONTENTS

INTRODUCTION

Introducing what is probably one of the best anthologies of short stories ever published,[1] V. S. Pritchett has written:

> For myself, the short story springs from a spontaneously poetic as distinct from a prosaic impulse — yet is not 'poetical' in the sense of a shuddering sensibility. Because the short story has to be succinct and has to suggest things that have been 'left out', are, in fact, there all the time, the art calls for a mingling of the skills of the rapid reporter or traveller with an eye for incident and an ear for real speech, the instincts of the poet and ballad-maker, and the sonnet writer's concealed discipline of form. The writer has to cultivate the gift for aphorism and wit. A short story is always a disclosure, often an evocation — as in Lawrence or Faulkner — frequently the celebration of character at bursting point: it approaches the mythical.

And writing elsewhere[2] about the Irish short story in particular, Pritchett remarks:

> What has always struck me in Irish writing is the sense of Ireland itself, its past or its imagined future, as a presence or invisible extra character in the story I am reading.

Linking these two observations of a writer who is himself a master of the modern short story, a question is automatically begged: why is it that the Irish possess what might be described as a genius for this particular literary pursuit? Reasons have been variously advanced: that due to disaffection, poverty, and the confusion of two languages Ireland was unable to provide the emergent nineteenth-century novel with the leisurely, stratified society which nurtured it so fruitfully in

1. *The Oxford Book of Short Stories* (O.U.P.).
2. Preface to *New Irish Writing*, ed. David Marcus (Quartet Books).

Victorian England; that the Irish mood is psychologically better suited by the shorter form; that we have, as a people, so inordinate a passion for gossipy anecdote that we are led quite naturally to the shorter form.

Be all that as it may, the fact remains that we have taken to our hearts the breathless gallop as opposed to the marathon. The ancient tale — often incorporating our legends, myths and parables — has made way without fuss for the modern story, which Elizabeth Bowen has called 'a child of this century'. There is a discenible development, a discernible connection between the two, even though the traditional mould was so determinedly shattered by Chekov, Joyce and Katherine Mansfield: on the surface at least everything now seems different but ancient or modern, the Irish short story is honoured all over the world, and for that reason alone no practitioner of quality should be allowed to slip through the literary net. I knew nothing of Margaret Barrington until I read the contents of this present volume. Having done so, I am convinced that it would be a shame, and a real loss, if her sharp, unique voice had died with her.

What she has perfectly understood in these eighteen stories is that her art is the art of the glimpse. She catches the moment, she possesses Pritchett's 'instinct of the poet and the ballad-maker'; and her stories are rich in his disclosures and evocations, and his sense of Ireland. They tell as little as they dare, craftily withholding information: in 'Fear', for instance, a story about rats, what is withheld is not unlike the heavy fat which weighs down the fashionable novel *Watership Down*. The regime and order of an animal kingdom, so laboriously revealed in that long book, is suggested in a couple of pages of the Barrington story — and long after it has been read the imagination continues to work.

What is most impressive about the writing of Margaret Barrington — apart from the power and intensity of certain individual stories — is its variation of mood. There is the ferocity of 'Village without Men. . .' and the harshness of 'David's Daughter, Tamar'. 'The Pedlar and the Lady' leaves behind it a chill melancholy, 'Homecoming' a taste of bitterness. There's a light-hearted reminder of O. Henry in 'There's One Born Every Minute', very different from the effect achieved in what is possibly the finest story in the collection, 'The Death of My Father'.

This ability to slip so effortlessly from mood to mood is the hallmark of the real short-story writer. So, too, is the ability to combine economy with detail, and an instinct for the right form and shape, the right tone of voice, when considering how best to tell a story. That skill and that gift repeatedly enliven these pages.

William Trevor

Homecoming

The snow lay thick on the land; thick and even, for no wind had come to pile it into heavy drifts. It lay white, soft and untrodden on the railway bank at the other side of the station, throwing its light upward so that the eyes were lifted with the light and saw the blackened beams and drifting cobwebs, untouched and undisturbed this many a year. The beechwoods which flanked the rising hill bore the heavy burden on their delicate tracery and the paths which entered them looked like dark rivers rushing underground. The sky hung down, grey, quiet, full of snow.

To the left, partly hidden by the trees, stood my father's mill, the whiteness of the roof melting into the surrounding whiteness. Now that the train had grumbled and hissed its way out of the station, I could hear the rattling noise of the machinery. A path, the snow piled high on either side, led to the mill from the station. I stood and looked along it, to see if my father were coming. But there was no sign of him. Already the last cold-pinched traveller had passed the barrier. I walked towards the hunched ticket-collector.

'Has Mr. Delahaie been here?' I asked.

''Deed no, Miss, he hasn't been about since I came on.'

I put down my bag and looked out with distaste at the snow-covered road. My town shoes were no protection and there did not seem to be any car for hire. What could have happened? Had they received my letter and wire? Was my mother ill? Was my sister dead?

I turned to the ticket collector who was hovering round like a distressed spirit, waiting for me to go away.

'Do you know if my sister is any worse?' I asked. In this small town everyone knew what happened.

'No worse, Miss, thank God. This very mornin' I seed Rachel Nielson. Her sister works at the Mill House. She was saying there was no change. It's queer now, isn't it, the way some has til suffer and some doesn't, in this world. It sets ye wonderin'.'

'Well, I'd best be getting along.'

'Leave yer bag, Miss, an' I'll bring it up mysel' when I go for me tea.'

I shook my head. I did not wish to enter my father's house empty-handed.

'Thanks, but it's not heavy,' I said and stepped out.

The snow struck cold through my shoes. A dank mist, heavy with snow, caught the lungs like an icy blow. I struggled along, past the Church, round the school corner and along the road to my father's house, miserable and depressed. Overhead the beech trees met in an arch, the snow nestling on the branches in high hummocks. All was silent. No bird moved. No creature stirred in the depths of the fields. No man walked abroad. I was alone.

The windows of my father's house shone brightly even on this dark day. The brass knocker shone. The steps were swept of snow and pipeclayed. The hall, when the parlour-maid opened the door, shone clean and cold as if wind-swept of every particle of dust. The house smelt heavily of beeswax. I remembered again how clean and cold that house had always been.

As I stepped into the hall and put down my bag, my mother came out of the morning room. She looked as she had always done, bright and handsome. No grey yet in her fine auburn hair, no crow's feet around her eyes, no hardening of colour to tell of age. Tall and triumphant, she looked down on me.

As she laid her hands on my shoulders and bent to kiss me, I noticed that her fingers slid into the fur of my coat, feeling and appraising it.

'Are you cold, dear?' she asked. 'Take off your coat and come into the morning room. There is a good fire there. The fire hasn't been lit yet in the drawing room.'

Of course not, I thought. It's not three o'clock yet. The drawing-room fire was only lit an hour before tea-time.

She took the coat and ran her fingers lovingly over the soft fur. Fine, long, white hands, their only ornament a wedding-ring.

'It's a nice coat, a lovely coat. It was good of your husband to buy you a coat like that. Your father never bought me such a fine coat.'

'No one bought it for me, Mother. I earned it.'

'Don't you make your husband buy your clothes?'

'No, why should I? I don't buy his.'

I looked round the room. In its familiarity, its unchanged regularity, it seemed strange. If something had been shifted, it might not have seemed so foreign. There, over the side board, the rack held my father's riding-crops. There, in a row, in the same order, stood the tall silver cups his greyhounds had won, coursing. I remembered his bitter regret when Carne Girl had failed to lift the Waterloo Cup. And there at the end of the row, not much larger than an egg-cup, stood the little cup I had won at the local show with my Airedale bitch, Lassie. The furniture, the sporting prints, the curtains, nothing had changed.

'How is Carol?' I asked.

'Poor child, a little better today. But it won't be long now, I wrote to prepare you.'

'I can see her?'

'Yes, but warm yourself first.'

'Where is my father?' I asked.

My mother smiled. There was such knowledge in her smile that I was startled. I had seen this look on her face before, when, as a child, I had been in disgrace with my father. But now I had come home, expecting tears, grief, even anger, but not triumph.

'He's gone to Belfast to buy yarns.'

'And he knew I was coming?'

'Yes, he knew you were coming.'

'Why didn't Donnelly meet me with the car?'

'Your father left orders that Donnelly was not to take out the car today.'

I remembered the bag in the hall and cursed myself. Why

hadn't I left it at the railway station?

My mother moved restlessly around the room, rearranging the table, pushing a glass here, another there, polishing a fork on a napkin. And all the while she talked, talked as if to keep me from talking.

'It's been hard, dear, all these years. I've had to bear the brunt of the nursing myself. Carol couldn't bear anyone else to touch her. It's quite understandable, of course. But I've felt it. There were times when I thought I couldn't go on. But God gives us His strength when our own fails. So I've battled along for everyone's sake. I know how terrible it has been for the child, laid up when others were enjoying themselves, when her sisters were well and happy. It's fallen very hard on me, too. It's three years since I've had a holiday. I've scarcely put my nose out of the house in all this time. And of course, your father . . . .'

'Tell me, Mother, what is the matter with Carol? You've never given me a straight answer.'

'Consumption.'

'Then why did you say, when I asked you three years ago, that she hadn't got it?'

'How could we be sure, dear? I couldn't just believe it.'

'If you had taken her out of this infernal climate, she might have recovered.'

My mother's mouth set in anger. But her eyes gleamed triumphantly.

'You will leave it to me to decide what is best for my own children. When you have children of your own, you can talk.'

I shrugged my shoulders. It was too late now to do anything.

'I'll run up and see her now.'

'Lunch will be served at any moment. I gave orders to serve it as soon as you arrived.'

'I won't be a second.'

My sister looked very small in the wide mahogany bed. Her frail body made scarcely a line under the bedclothes. The carefully brushed black curls made the boniness of her face all the more pathetic. Her large grey eyes were dark and tragic. I noticed with a lump in my throat the gay coquettry of her ribbons, her silk nightgown. And her hands, thin and large-jointed, lay on the cover, the nails carefully manicured and varnished.

The cheek beneath my lips was hot and burning. She breathed shortly and quickly.

'See,' I said, 'I have a present for you. I couldn't think what to bring you and I was in a hurry. It's a little Chinese coat.'

'Thank you, oh thank you,' she said. I saw that in her manner and way of speaking she had stayed a little girl, had refused to grow up.

She caressed the padded coat with long bony hands, just as my mother had caressed my coat. She laid it beside her on the bed and continued to caress it.

'Wouldn't you like to put it on?' I asked.

'Later, perhaps.' She looked me over carefully. 'You look very well. Thinner than you were. Or maybe it's that dark dress. Why didn't you wear a blue dress. You look pretty in blue. Do you remember that blue dress of yours I always wanted? And when you gave it to me, it didn't suit me. It was such a pretty dress and I couldn't understand why it didn't look nice on me when it looked nice on you. Blue isn't my colour.'

'No, but then I could never wear red.'

'No, you could never wear red.'

Down below in the hall the maid was sounding the gong.

'I must go now. I'll be back presently.'

'Don't let Mother keep you talking. She'll try to, you know.'

'I'll hurry back. I promise.'

'Well, what do you think of her?' asked my mother as I sat down to the overladen table.

'She seems very frail.'

My mother sighed.

'I'll be lonely when she's gone.'

'You have two other children.'

'Ah, but you're married and away and Helen is still at school. No one can take Carol's place.'

This conversation could go on interminably if someone did not stop it.

'I wonder if I could have a little whiskey, Mother?' I

asked. 'The train was cold and draughty.'

'Certainly my dear, if you feel you need it.' She went to the sideboard and took out the decanter. 'I hope,' she eyed me critically as I poured the drink into a wineglass, 'that you don't make a habit of it.'

'No, Mother, I'm like Father, I've no taste for strong waters.'

'It's bad for people with your tendency.'

'My tendency?'

'This tendency to consumption which comes from your father's family, of course. None of my people ever had it.'

So Father was being blamed for that.

'You've lost weight,' she remarked.

'Just the plumpness of youth.'

'Do you eat enough? Nowadays girls save on their stomachs to put it on their backs. They pay for it later on.'

'The only thing I suffer from, Mother, is a tendency to indigestion, due to overfeeding in my youth.'

My mother could never bear even the shadow of criticism.

'No one can say,' her colour rose, her voice sharpened, 'no one, that you did not get of the best. I keep the best table in Ulster, and that means in Ireland.'

'That's just what I'm saying, Mother. We were all overfed like Strassbourg geese, until our livers rebelled.'

'You were always bilious,' said my mother. 'You take that from your father, too.'

I wondered why I and my mother were always at cross purposes. No conversation could go easily and amiably. I felt I was as much to blame as she was. I could be tactful with all the world except my own mother. Now, since I could find nothing tactful to say, I fell silent, knowing well that my mother would put my silence down to sulkiness.

But she could not keep silent. She had not seen me for three years and she had a great deal to complain of.

'Your father,' she said, 'is becoming more and more difficult. With all I've gone through, you'd think he would be more considerate of my feelings. He doesn't seem to mind how he hurts me and his tempers are getting worse. He lives completely alone now, closes himself up with his books. I don't believe he understands a word that's in them. I tried to read one and it just doesn't make sense. They're all about religion and philosophy. He's very interested in religion. I would have thought it might have softened him.'

'It has never been noted for that.'

'What is it for then? I can see you are still irreligious. Some day you'll know better. Some day you'll discover that your parents were right. Let us hope it will not be too late.'

'How are you off for money?' I asked, simply to turn the subject.

'What about money? Your father is getting worse. I don't know what he does with his money. He doesn't give it to me. He makes scenes over the bills. I can't run this house any cheaper than I do. I defy anyone to do it. It's been run as it always was, as my mother's house was run. Only the very best comes in here. I'm not one to give the servants margarine and eat butter myself, like many another.'

That I knew was true. Even my mother's servants suffered from bilious attacks.

'But you know, darling,' I said and I could not help laughing at her earnestness, 'you and I don't really need all this.'

I waved my hand towards the roast chicken and boiled ham, the ragout simmering on the hot-plate, the four dishes of vegetables, the chicory salad, the sauces.

'Not a bite will be wasted.'

'I know, my dear. When your husband and your children refuse further stuffing, you stuff the servants, and when they can't take any more, you call in one of the men from the yard and feed him. It's charming, darling, but it's horribly extravagant.'

'I don't hold with economy in food. Look at me. I eat well. If I didn't could I stand up to all I have to do? I'm forty-six now. I haven't a wrinkle or a grey hair. I hope you'll be half the woman your mother is now, at my age.'

'I'm sure I won't, dear.'

'Well, child, as I was saying, I don't know what he does with his money. It's a shocking way for a wife to be. I haven't a notion what comes in or what goes out. I don't know what he has saved or if he has saved. God knows I've been a good wife. Is that any way to treat me?'

I was silent. This hopeless, everlasting wrangling over money in a house which could not be poor, was something I could never understand.

'And he's getting worse. Meaner and stingier every day. I ask you, child, where is the money going to? There used to be plenty. Of course I don't know, but I have my suspicions. I had brothers of my own and I know what men are like.'

Suddenly a great pity for my mother filled my heart. She loved my father so much, so jealously and had to live these years side by side with his indifference. I saw now that her nagging, her obstinacy, her rows were because she felt better when he was stirred to some active passion, even hatred. Remorselessly she sacrificed everything to her feeling for my father; her peace, her pride, her servants, her children. Even Carol — for she would not leave him to take the child away. Everything except her house. That stood for her very existence.

'Don't worry,' I patted her hand. 'Business may be bad. Linen isn't what it was.'

'Is your husband difficult about money?'

'No. We just lump everything together into one fund.'

'My poor girl! How awful! Then he must know everything you spend.

'We neither of us worry.'

'I'll send you a pound or two now and then but you must not say anything to him about it. I can always manage to get a few pounds out of the housekeeping money.'

'No, no Mother, I have plenty.'

'I've made your favourite pudding. I went down to the kitchen specially to prepare it this morning. A crème caramel. I remembered how you always liked it.'

'But Mother dear, I'm full of food.'

'Nonsense, it can't hurt you. It's made of fresh eggs and milk and cream 'Twill do you good.'

I laughed. 'Darling, you are sweet when you talk about food.'

Her face softened. 'I often worry about you and wonder if you eat enough. You're a good child. I often think it strange that you, who turned out the worst, should have the kindest heart.'

'Maybe that's why.'

But now she was back on her grievances. She worried at them like a scutching mill.

'Do you know, Carol has got just like your father. She saves every penny. She's got money hidden in that bed and I can never find it. I turn it over and search — but not a sign.'

'Poor child!'

'She's getting so cunning about getting money out of people. I know for certain that Mr. Edgington gives her five pounds when he comes over to see us. To buy herself books, he says. And no one ever sees it again. If your father knew, he'd kill us all.'

'Don't let him know. Stuff her with money if it makes her happy.'

'My dear,' said my mother, 'that is neither a wise nor a nice thing to say.'

I went upstairs again to talk to Carol.

She is my sister, I thought, as I wandered round the room. My sister — of the same flesh and blood as I am. Yet she is a stranger. I scarcely know her. And because she is of my flesh and blood, I am moved, saddened, to see her die. Does blood, does family mean so much, that the fate of this almost unknown girl should distress me? To distract my thoughts and amuse her, I talked of places I had been since I last saw her.

'This time last year, I was in Nice, Carol. You should see Nice. Sunshine. Dark orange groves with bright fruit. Fields of flowers. Palm trees waving against the blue sky. You lie in the sun and remember all the famous people who have sailed over that blue sea; Ulysses, Jason, Hannibal, Nelson. Even our great-uncle who was Admiral of the Mediterranean fleet.'

'I know. But no one has ever heard of him outside the family.'

I laughed. 'And we heard plenty. You must come there with me when you are better.'

'That would be nice.' Her grey eyes smiled the ever hopeful smile of the consumptive.

I looked out of the window. Down below stretched the long terraced garden, white with snow, and in the hollow by the stream the bleaching greens, backed by the mounting slope of trees reaching into the grey of the sky. When I had been here last, these trees had been green against the white and blue of June and the greens had been white, too, white with long strips of linen.

Out of the greyness the fine snowflakes were beginning to fall. I turned away shivering and began to admire the pretty room, the books, the pictures, the flowers and asked: 'Carol, you have everything you want?'

She raised her head from the pillows with difficulty and looked around. The cords of her neck stood out as they do on the neck of an old man.

'I need a new bedside lamp. That one is so ugly. It doesn't match the room.'

'It doesn't,' I agreed. 'Now, shall I have one sent to you or shall I give you the money and ask some firm in London to send you a catalogue. You could have a good time picking one out for yourself.'

'Give me the money.'

She stretched out her bony hand, the long stick of an arm, and took the money. Quickly it disappeared beneath the bed-clothes as if she were afraid that I might snatch it back. I felt, as I am sure old Mr. Edgington felt, that I was buying off the Danes of a guilty conscience.

'Tell me, Carol, why did Father not wish to meet me?'

The grey eyes looked fearlessly into mine.

'He's angry with you.'

'I know that. But his rage has had three years to cool down. There must be something else.'

'Mother told him.'

'Told him what?'

'That you had been living with your husband before you married him.'

'Now, how did she find that out? And why did she tell him?'

'You know, she tells him everything against us. Specially against you. But when she told him she was frightened. I know, because for days she would hardly leave me.'

'Why?'

'Oh, you know what he is. He got into one of his tempers — but worse, far worse, than any before. He wanted to kill you, but he wanted to kill her, too. He shouted and stormed all over the place and he didn't speak to anyone for three weeks. He never even came to see me. Helen was home and she sat in the corner and cried and trembled. We all talked in whispers. It was horrible.'

'So that's it,' I said. 'Why does Mother have to do this when she knows what's going to happen?'

But I knew why my mother did it. I knew that after these tempests of rage and black sullen silence, my father turned to her, penitent and submissive. For a few days the cold indifference was banished. He lay in her hands like an egg. Then she would push her children away from her, make strange with them, rebuke them, treat them as infants. 'Go away,' she would say. 'I want to be alone with your father.'

'I knew it couldn't be true.'

'But what if it were, Carol?'

'Things like that don't happen to us. Only to mill-girls.'

'They happen even to queens.'

'Not to us. Not to us.' She panted and a light perspiration broke out on her forehead, on her upper lip.

'Don't talk so much, dear. I shouldn't let you talk.'

I began to chatter about London, the shops and the restaurants, theatres and plays I had seen. Suddenly she asked: 'Are you happy?'

'Yes, dear, why?'

'You don't look very happy. Do you mind if I ask? Does your husband beat you?'

'Good heavens, no, child. What put such a notion into your head?'

'I often dream that he does. I can see it all so clearly in the dream.'

'Well, it's all nonsense. It would never enter his head.'

'I see it all so plainly. Mother says he was a soldier, a common soldier and then a gunman.'

'Don't listen to Mother. She talks a lot of nonsense. Dear Carol,' I took her hand, 'I won't say he's perfect. But he's not cruel. He's much kinder than my own family really. He wouldn't do such a thing. He loves me. He spoils me horribly. Look at these pretty shoes, at my silk stockings, at this dress. They are all expensive. I've got a fur coat downstairs. Would he have given me all these things if he were not kind?'

'I'm glad,' she said and sighed.

'Now promise not to think of this again.'

'I promise.'

I was holding her thin, hot hand in mine when my mother entered the room. Again I was conscious of her air of triumph and I knew the cause. She had finally separated me from my father.

'My dear,' she said. 'I'm sorry but you'll have to go if you don't want to miss your train.'

'Goodbye, sweet,' I said to Carol and bent to kiss her. 'Get better and come to see me soon.'

Her grey eyes looked into mine so fearlessly, so proudly, so apart.

'It is too late, now,' she said.

In the hall I said to my mother: 'Mother, please, when you are talking with Carol, will you tell her that my husband gave me this coat, these shoes, these gloves. Tell her that, for her sake.'

My mother was almost in tears.

'Oh, my child,' she said brokenly. 'To have to let you go. To have to let you go on such a night. Your coat will be ruined.'

Without another word, without kissing her goodbye, I lifted my bag and went out into the soft, swirling snow.

At the station I went into the waiting room to wait for the train which was late and to shake the snow from my clothes. A middle aged woman was standing in front of the fire, a steaming foot on the fender. Her face was pinched and grey with cold and she held her threadbare coat wrapped tightly round her body. She stepped aside when I entered the room.

'Stay where you are,' I said, 'I'm not cold.'

'It's brave and cold the night,' she said, and watched me as I shook my coat, watched me with interest but no envy. Yet what right had I to a warm coat when she had none. I opened my bag to get out a book and saw the scarf I had bought for my mother and forgotten. I held it out to the woman.

'Look,' I said. 'I bought this for my mother and she did not like it. If I bring it across the border I'll have to pay duty and it's not worth it. Maybe it might help to keep out the cold. Would you care for it?'

The hands that took the scarf were bony like my sister's, large knuckled like hers, but the nails were not manicured. They were black and broken with heavy labour. The woman stood on tiptoe and looked into the large fly-blown mirror. She tied the scarf round her neck, twisting her head from side to side, arranged and rearranged the knot. She smiled happily to herself and patted the scarf, forgetting her thin coat and broken shoes. Again I felt I was buying off the Danes. Then she rolled those thin, work-worn hands in the ends of the scarf, she turned to me with a happy smile and said: "Eh, it's grand. It's boony dear. Thankye, daughter!"

There is peace and reconciliation in the idiom of the people. I could hear the train whistling as it came out of the tunnel. I turned to go out onto the platform.

Fear

Have you ever known what it is to be afraid? I don't speak of
the ordinary fears which beset us day and night, or those silly
fears which survive from infancy and cannot be reasoned out
of our systems. I mean primitive fear, a fear which throws
you back on yourself as your sole protection. Well, if you
ever have, you'll never be afraid of anything again. It is a
fear which casteth out fear.

One day I got a letter from a lawyer informing me that I
had inherited a small estate in the north-west of Donegal.
This estate which for hundreds of years had been the
property of my family had until lately been in the possession
of an uncle whom no one seemed to know. He lived all alone
in the old house and refused to hold any communication
with any of his relatives. And so surly was his nature that
they had all long since given up trying to do anything with
him. He was only a name to the younger members of the
family — Uncle Joss — a kind of bogie man whom we used to
picture with one leg, a squint and a large ferocious beard. As
we grew older we simply forgot that Uncle Joss ever existed.
He belonged to the same category as Father Christmas, Blue-
beard, and His Satanic Majesty. As he could no longer be
used for disciplinary purposes he just died a natural death.

And here at last he had really died and left me the old
home. How he had ever come to know my name will always
remain a mystery to me. I don't really think he did. I imagine
he just thought that maybe one or two of his nephews or
grand-nephews would have been dowered with the family
name of Josslin, so he put it down, hoping thereby to cause

some confusion. But as luck would have it, Uncle Joss had been so unpopular that I was the only Josslin Osborne, so to me fell the family estate, three hundred acres of land, most of it unfit for anything but shooting and sheep-grazing, and an old house which had withstood the storms of three hundred years.

I was twenty-three years of age at this time, a third-year medical student. I had just come to the momentous decision that it was time for me to stop playing around and to think of doing some work. So providing myself with a new fishing-rod and riding-kit, my father's old sporting rifle and a few medical books, I set off for my estate.

As the house was forty miles Irish from a railway station I bought an old Ford car, put my bags, books and an assortment of tinned food, bought by my mother who seemed afraid of my starving in the wilds, into the back and one fine July day I drove off.

It took the best part of three days to get there. I know this sounds incredible but you should have seen the roads, some of them no better than donkey tracks. Still those old Fords, you remember them, built up in the air and rattling like a ghost's false teeth — well, they'd take anything except the side-wall of a house. You had only to fill them up with juice and point their noses at it. Finally, a bit shaken and rather in a mess, I arrived at the market town of Drum. The keys of the old house were with the local solicitor, a Mr. Silas Cloughery.

I made my way up the rather squalid street, passed three combined public houses and grocery shops and drew up with a rattle outside the house and office of Mr. Cloughery. No one appeared to notice my arrival. I went up to the door and knocked. No one came. I turned the handle and went in. A vague sound of voices came from a room on the left-hand side of the hall. I rapped with my knuckles. An angry voice answered me: 'Can't ye come in? Have ye got no legs on ye?'

I entered. There with his back to the mantlepiece stood Mr. Cloughery busily declaiming to the world in general and his clerk in particular. Tall and thin with a face prematurely wrinkled from indigestion, he was one of those men who are eternally angry about something. The existence of other people in the world is in itself an offence, and he let

them know it. With the sure instinct which seems to guide all
ill-tempered people, he had chosen as his clerk an underfed
young boy who looked as if he could not say boo to a goose
as the saying goes. He certainly would never have attempted
to say boo to Mr. Cloughery, and in the presence of strangers
he hung his head like a love-sick loon and spoke from under
the shelter of his eyebrows. It appeared that I had
interrupted a flow of eloquence on the part of Mr. Cloughery
as to what the world was coming to. Very annoyed he looked
at me and said, almost shouted: 'Well! And well now, what
do you want?'

'My name,' I replied, 'is Osborne.'

'Well, and what if it is? What has that to do with me?'
remarked Mr. Cloughery, still very irate.

'I've called,' I said, as quietly as I could,' for the keys of
my house.'

'Now have you indeed?' said Mr. Cloughery in his best
court-room manner. 'And do you mean to insinuate that I
may have taken your keys?'

'I mean to insinuate nothing,' I replied, getting a trifle
annoyed myself. 'But I was given to understand that the
keys of my late uncle's house, Drum Manor, were left in your
possession, and I am asking you to hand them over. I am his
grand-nephew, Josslin Osborne.'

Mr. Cloughery's manner changed. I don't mean to say that
it became any less legal and overbearing but a shade of
astonishment came into his sallow face. He gasped slightly
and looked at me as if I were something in the nature of a
natural wonder.

'You're not thinking,' he ejaculated, 'you're surely not
thinking of going out there?'

'And why not?'

Mr. Cloughery hesitated.

'Well, then, I wouldn't,' he said after a pause.

I became very irritated. This man was a bore and a
nuisance. 'Give me the keys if you have them,' I said gruffly,
'And perhaps you could let me have someone with me to
show me the way.'

'Sure, sure, I'll give you the keys, young man, but still
I'd advise you to stop here. If it's fishing you want, well,

Mrs. Mullins up on the hill will make ye comfortable enough. Ye won't have anyone to look after ye out there.'

'Had my uncle no servants?'

'Not what ye'd call servants. There was an old sailor who looked after him, but your uncle provided for him so he's gone up to Derry to live with a married daughter. There's nobody would go next or near the place.'

'Why? Is it haunted?'

'It might be and again it mightn't. I never heard anything said about it's being haunted. But still and all it has a very bad name.'

I shrugged my shoulders.

'What about it?' I remarked, 'I'm not afraid of a bad name. It never hurt anyone. Please find the keys and someone to drive up there with me.'

Mr. Cloughery looked at me gloomily and shook his head. 'Get the keys, Sam. They're in the back room in a box labelled Drum Manor. And now maybe,' he continued more amiably opening a cupboard at the side of the fireplace, 'you'd like a wee drop to keep up your heart.'

I thanked him and accepted though it was still early in the afternoon.

'If ye take my advice,' he said grimly, 'ye'll stop off at Doherty's and buy yourself some of the best. Ye might need it out there.' In rural middle-class circles whiskey is never mentioned by its name. It is always referred to as 'some of the best', or 'the wine of the country' or 'something to wet your whistle'. I have even heard it called 'the saviour of mankind'. But never whiskey. The clerk came back and we departed. We were speeded on our way by the gloomy solicitor who shouted after me: 'Mind now that ye stop off at Doherty's and say I sent ye. He'll give ye decent stuff.'

I stopped off and then we rattled up the hill again and out into the country. Up that mountain-side, round hair-raising corners rattled the old Lizzie, never stopping to take breath though by her grunts she seemed to need it. When at last we topped the rise, the shy young clerk pointed across the valley to a square house of grey granite and said: 'Yonder's Drum Manor!'

I stopped the car and looked. It was certainly a marvellous

situation even though the grey house looked a trifle for-
bidding. Behind it were the usual stunted sycamores of the
region, blown over to one side by the western gales. But
stretching out before it was the open sea with Tory Island
rising like a castle on the horizon. On the other side rose the
great Derryveigh Mountains with their mica tops glittering in
the sun. Beyond it a blue lake, small and reed-grown, shone
like a mirror. Above all, the song of the larks in the clear air.
I felt like joining in their singing. The joy of possession was
mine. As I sat back there in the car I could see the first
Osborne putting in here from Norway thinking that at last
he had found a haven after many days at sea. He never left
it, and here was I — I, Josslin Osborne, coming home, the
last of the Vikings. I let my imagination roam for a few
minutes. My daydream was interrupted by the young clerk.

'Would it be too much to ask of you, sir, to let me turn
back now. Ye canna miss the way, it leads straight past the
avenue. It would be a long road home for me. I'd best make
it back now.'

I thanked him and let him go but the daydream had
vanished. I started up the car again and twenty minutes later
I drew up before my ancestral home.

Never shall I forget the sight that met my eyes when I
opened the door. During my lifetime I had seen many
delapidated houses, there are many in Ireland, but never such
a one. For here were all the signs of the elegance of a bygone
time. The high walls, panelled with wood washed up from the
sea, wood in which one could trace here and there the mark
of the sea-worm, silken curtains tattered like the flags over
the cathedral choir, the hearth-places with the dead ashes
which had lain there since God knows when, and the elegant
gilt furniture, pieces of hand-painted satin-wood, stood
around, decrepid, broken, — just junk. The oil paintings of
my ancestors hung in ribbons from their frames. The
upholstery of the chairs and the carpets were in holes and
lumps of horse-hair lay about the rooms. Desolation was
written all over the place.

I went from room to room. Everything smelt of decay
and the salt damp of the sea. I tried to open a window and
broke it in the process. So I opened all the doors instead.

At last I arrived at the back of the house and there over-looking a square courtyard and an old Italian garden gone completely wild, I found a room, the strangest room I'd ever seen.

It must have been the room generally known as the library, though the only books in it were a copy of the Holy Bible and two books — one entitled *The Horse* and the other *Deep Sea Fishing.* Instead of the high oak or mahogany panels, here the room was encased in sheet tin, ceiling, walls and floor. A large bed stood in the middle of the room and a closed stove occupied the fireplace. A table, a chair and some pots comprised the rest of the furniture. Evidently my uncle had used this as his last camping place. I took an instant dis-like to the room and set about establishing myself in one of the others. I chose the drawing-room because of its fine view over the sea towards Tory. I dragged my uncle's bed in there and made a fire. By the time evening was falling, I had made the room look as habitable as possible. I lit the lamp, placed it on the most secure of the tables and getting into bed, proceeded to read myself to sleep.

I do not remember blowing out the lamp but I must have done so for when I awoke the room was in darkness. I awoke suddenly as if startled from sleep, my senses all alive. Was there someone in the room? I knew that tramps had a way of using uninhabited houses. I listened. This was not the sound of human beings. There was a scuffling, a rushing round and then some squeaks. Mice, I thought. Well, tomorrow I'll get a good terrier and a cat and that'll settle them. Maybe lay down some virus. Damn them they'll stop me from getting to sleep. I turned towards the table beside the bed and groped for the matches. I struck a light and then — I saw what was causing this commotion. A large rat jumped down from my bed. I looked around the room. The whole place was a seething mass of grey animals, pushing, shoving, squeaking, jumping from tables and chairs. The very floor seemed to move as if in an earthquake. Bright specks of light, hundreds of small, glittering eyes pierced the gloom. In terror I let drop the burned-out match. It had scorched my fingers.

Crouching up in the bed, I lit the lamp and looked about again. The rats were gathering in the far end of the room like an army. I looked frantically round for a means of escape. I could see none. The horde lay between me and the door and windows. Then I looked for a weapon. My eyes lit on my riding boots, my beautiful new riding boots, the pride of my heart. I had placed them carefully the night before just beside my bed. I pulled them on and stepped out on to the floor. Two steps and I was beside the fireplace and had seized the poker.

When I turned to face them they did not run away. I stood with my back to the wall and waited. After two or three minutes, incredibly long minutes, they advanced, suddenly, treacherously, like an army corps. I did not realize it until they were surging around me, biting my boots, jumping up at me, snarling like dogs as I beat them back again and again. I had good reason to praise the leather Mr. Buchanan had put into those boots.

Horrible and fearful pictures ran through my mind. I remembered the gruesome story of a bishop, yes Bishop Hatto in his Rat-House on the Rhine. I remembered terrible stories told me by servants in my childhood, by those good, kind Irish nannies who never fear the consequences of their ghostly tales. But none of these stories took real shape in my mind. They just flashed through it like the pictures on a newsreel while I brought down the heavy poker again and again.

Suddenly the room cleared. They vanished as if through the walls, which in fact they did. When I examined the room I discovered the old panelling full of rat-holes. I crept back to bed. There was nothing but the dead bodies of the enemy to remind me that it had not all been a horrible nightmare. Why had they vanished like that, all in a body? I did not fall asleep until morning when the grey light of dawn brought back some confidence.

I awoke in broad daylight. I sat up in bed and tried to think. I noticed that I moved in a slow sleep-walking manner but that my brain worked with lightning rapidity. It is strange now, looking back on it, that the thought of running away or of getting help never entered my mind. I was far too frightened. I dressed slowly, made some lunch, and then wandered round the house. I brought in my father's old rifle.

I found I had no ammunition with me, but the butt-end of a gun is a good weapon. I placed it beside the bed. I never moved from the house all day.

It is strange that all the emotions, hatred, love, fear, greed, desire when they reach their height resemble one another, result in the same ecstasy. All that day I went about like a man in a dream, like a man in love for the first time. I felt, too, all the secrecy of first love. If someone had come to the door, I believe I would have said nothing at all about all this. I was barely aware of my surroundings. My legs moved, my arms moved but without any conscious effort on my part. I was like a puppet in a play, moved by strings and not by the movements of my brain. But my mind was feverishly alive. The processes of thought were clear, logical, all-embracing. So the day passed.

When evening came I made myself a good meal, dressed myself in riding-boots and breeches and a leather golf jacket, climbed on to the bed, turned down the lamp until it was a mere flicker which gave no light and waited.

Soon they began to gather. There was the scratching and squeaking, the running and leaping that I had heard the night before. I leant forward and turned up the light. I leaped out of bed and took up my position near the fireplace.

It seemed to me that for every rat there had been the night before there were now ten. But this may have been the result of an excited imagination. Again they waited as if expecting me to charge them. But seeing that I stood there on the defensive they came on. I kept beating them back with the butt-end of the rifle. I could feel the hair on my head rise like that of a terrier dog and cold shivers ran over my body but I fought with skill and concentration. I never aimed without bringing home the blow. And I moved slowly, wasting no effort. I knew that they could not bite through or tear that leather and my breeches saved my legs when they jumped.

Still on they came. Just as I cleared a space around me it was filled up again. Then suddenly they retreated towards the far end of the room and I noticed something. For as I say my brain was very active and receptive at that moment. They gathered round one rat who seemed to be directing

the proceedings. He was a giant of a rat, very strong and
active. I thought — if I can bring that fellow down, I've won.

I looked about me. The rats advanced again. I swung the
rifle. Down it came again and again. I glanced up. There was
their leader, their king, rushing around in the background
making noises and apparently directing operations, encourag-
ing his troop to advance.

For a moment I stopped. The enemy bit and snarled like
dogs at my heels. I took a careful look around. There on the
mantlepiece I saw a white, china ball, about the size of a
cricket ball, one of those useless ornaments with which our
grandmothers used to decorate their mantlepieces. I took it
up and paying no heed to the surging mass around me I
aimed it.

It hit him fair and square. He went down under it and
never stirred, never even squeaked. I stood there motionless,
looking across the room at him, heedless of my surroundings.
A terrible feeling of relief rose up in me and I felt as if someone had taken a tight iron band from my head. Strangely
enough my thoughts and plans became confused. I do not
remember noticing it but suddenly the room was empty and
there was I standing with one hand on the mantlepiece, alone
in the room. I let the rifle drop, and put my trembling right
hand to my forehead. It was wet with sweat as if I had come
out of a river. I went over to the bed, dropped down on it
and fell asleep.

It was early morning when I awoke. For the first time I
heard the song of the birds. The sun was peeping over the
shoulder of Mount Aghla. I went to the window and
wrenched it wide open. The sound of water, running water,
the boom of the waves on the distant bar, the high shrill
song of the larks in the clear morning air, they all flowed
into my consciousness like a healing drink.

Then a movement on the lawn attracted my attention. I
looked. Through the rough grass moved an army of rats away
from the house. They moved like a sea, hundreds of them. I
watched them. A sadness came over me, like the sadness one
feels when one's beloved steals away in the grey light of
dawn.

They were making for the little stream which flowed

along at the bottom of the lawn. First came the big strong ones, singly. They were followed by the mass of the others and the stragglers, the old and very young in the rear. Then I noticed a strange thing.

There were three of them. They had a long straw in their mouths. The two outer ones were young and strong, and they were leading an old, blind rat. Then I knew that my house was once again my own. They had really left me, bringing with them their old and maimed, leaving me in triumph with their dead.

It was to be

The woman threw open the dining-room door, entered and placed the basket on the hearth-rug. A man followed with two suit-cases which he dropped behind her.

'Just leave the trunks out on the steps,' said the woman. 'It's a fine day. I can unpack them there and carry the clothes and books upstairs. They're very heavy.'

'Will that be all then?' asked the man. He stood in the doorway, a small red-headed man with light-grey eyes and a sallow face. He hesitated as if he had no wish to go.

'I think so,' said the woman, opening her hand-bag. She, too, hesitated and looked round the room. 'Do you mind carrying the wireless in here? The square cardboard box. And perhaps you could send someone up from the village to fix it up for me.'

'I'll do it now for ye if ye like,' said the man briskly. 'I do a bit of that sort of thing. In this part of the world ye can't live by drivin' a car, even if ye cud get the petrol. Ye have to turn yer hand to many a thing.'

'Fine! I'll go out to the kitchen, unpack some stores and make us a cup of tea. But first I must let His Lordship out.'

The man stood and watched her as she unfastened the lid of the wicker basket. Inside a large cat lay on some wood shavings.

'A fine cat!' he said.

The cat stretched his paws, stuck his head over the side of the basket, yawned largely and got up. He was a large grey tom-cat with a white chest and stomach. His pointed ears were tufted like those of a lynx. He had no tail.

The man's prominent grey eyes stared at the cat.

'What's happened to him?' he asked.

'Nothing. Oh, do you mean the tail? He's never had one; he's a Manx cat.'

'It's not in nature. A bob-tailed cat!' The man's voice was full of doubt.

'It's a breed,' said the woman.

The cat swayed on his long legs, stretched again and began an investigation of the man's trouser-legs.

'I was never one to set much store on cats,' he said and edged away uneasily. The cat turned disdainfully and followed his mistress out of the room.

When the woman came back from the kitchen with the tray, not only was the aerial up but a can of fresh milk stood on the table.

'I called across the field to Mary-Ellen Hegarty for it,' the man explained. 'An' she said as how, if ye were to let her know how much ye wanted, she'd send along Corny with it in the morning.'

'How kind you all are,' said the woman. 'And you have the aerial up already.'

'No bother. None at all. The car's a sort of workshop, ye know. I just happened to be bringing along some wire and insulators for Dr. MacManus.'

'But won't he be wanting them?'

'Ah — he can wait.'

The woman laughed gently. 'I've been away for so long,' she said softly. 'I've forgotten so much.'

The man drank down his tea, refused another cake and went back to his work. His small, narrow-chested figure bent over the wires. The woman noticed how deft and quick his small hands were. He chattered as he worked about the wireless, motoring difficulties, the weather, the best kind of potatoes for the garden, where she could get them.

'Are you worried much with rabbits here?' asked the woman.

'Not so much now they're fetching half a crown a piece on account of the war in England.' He spoke as some do of the war in China. Very remote. 'I never cared greatly for atin' rabbit meself,' he went on. 'They're onnatural craytures.' Here he looked modestly at the wall and lowered his voice almost to a whisper. 'They do say — savin' yer presence, ma'am — and mind ye I wudn't go bail for it — but they do say that in some parts of the country, down Crosshaven-way or East Cork maybe, that cats have gone to live in the burrows and bred there with the rabbits an' there's craytures there half one, half the other.' His large expressive eyes turned willy-nilly in the direction of the large tom-cat standing in the doorway, sniffing suspiciously. 'Mind ye, there's some as wud wear down their teeth talkin'.'

The woman rattled the china on the tray to hide the laughter which bubbled up in her throat. She moved to the window and looked down on the long green valley which stretched away from the orchard wall, patterned with small stone-walled fields, edged on either side by rough brown hills. In the hollow a small steel-grey lake winked in the winter sunshine.

'How lovely it is here. So peaceful, too. No aeroplanes; no bombs.'

'It's quiet enough, then. Too quiet, sometimes. Most of the young people have gone. You'll find it a great change. But then ye can have too much of the other thing. Were ye in the blitz, ma'am?'

'Yes, it was strange and terrible. When I looked at those ruined houses, those wrecked streets, I realized I was elderly and tired and useless; a burden. So I did as the children had been urging me to do. I came back home.'

'Ye did right. The graveyards are full of men with great courage and small sense.'

The cat began an inspection of the room. He smelled the chairs and table-legs, examined the grate. Then he sniffed along the skirting until he came to an empty corner. He backed away and growled. The hair on his back stood like a knife-edge and the little tuft where his tail should have been fluffed out stiffly. His ears turned back, his head flattened, he spat in the direction of the empty corner. He ran towards his mistress, climbed up the back of her chair and jumped on to her shoulder. She stroked and soothed him. The man looked at the cat with interest.

'He smells the crayture,' he said.

'What?' asked the woman.

'An attar it was called. A bit like a dog and a bit like a seal. It lived there with old Mr. Colbert.'

'An otter? Strange to keep an otter in the house. Who was this Mr. Colbert?'

'He was a quare man, very quare altogether. A Protestant clergyman. He'd been a chaplain in India an' it's how we thought he'd had a touch of the sun. He kep' this attar, a couple of dogs and a bull in the orchard for a pet. For what good is a bull to anyone but a farmer?'

'Are there any Protestants here?'

'Not now. But that never stalled Mr. Colbert. Every Sunday, sure as day dawned he'd go down and open the old church. The attar wud be hangin' roun' his neck like a lady's fur, an' the two dogs, one a small pom-dog and the other a big fella, wud trot along after him. He left the bull at home. Supposedly he cudn't get it through the church-door! The two dogs an' the attar ud sit there in the pews, quiet as Christians, while Mr. Colbert wud read the service and play a hymn and preach a sermon. A great preacher seemingly. He'd thump on the pulpit, an' shout at the two dogs and the attar to give up their sinful ways. Then they'd go home and he'd cook the dinner.

'Did he have no servant?'

'Wudn't let one next or nigh the place.' Again the modestly lowered voice. 'Savin' yer presence, ma'am, owin' to an objection he had to the female. He was as handy about the place as any woman. Still he was a likeable gentleman. But quare — no mistakin' it — quare.'

'What happened to them all?'

The man straightened himself and accepted another cup of tea.

'Ah, the way of all flesh. The old man died a year back. The bull was sold. The big dog died; just wudn't ate. A home was got for the other. And the attar. No-one seems to know rightly what come of the attar. Some say this, some that.'

'It probably found a home for itself in the river. It would be happier there than in any house.'

'True, too, ma'am. There now, that's all ready fixed for

ye. Wait a minit.'

He left the room and returned with a large battery. 'I'll leave ye this. It's Mrs. MacNamara's. Her other will hold out for a day or two more. I'll take yours along and get it charged for ye.'

'But, surely —'

'Now, never ye worry. She won't miss it. I'll say goodday to ye now, ma'am, an' if ye're wantin' any little thing doin', just ask for Mike Sullivan. They all know Mike.'

The woman accompanied him to the door. The little man looked at the big cat perched on her shoulder, his pale eyes full of misgiving.

'Ma'am, a cat like that — ' he said. 'A lady like you — maybe ye wudn't like a pom-dog?'

'I should love — No, I'm sorry. You see, His Lordship wouldn't like a dog.'

'I have a nice one wud just suit ye,' the little man sighed as he wriggled back under the driver's seat.

Through the unprotected windows of her bedroom the woman looked out on the shabby old garden, flooded with winter sunshine.

'See,' she cried to the cat. 'The garden. What a waste! Still, it's winter and all the flowers are dead. But look, there are snowdrops under the hedge and winter aconite. And there's a violet bed. Come along and pick a bunch of violets.'

She ran out into the garden. A heavy smell of decaying leaves hung over it. The paths were neglected and moss-grown. As she bent down to pick the flowers, the cat ran up the slope of her back and pressed his head against hers.

When darkness came the woman lit all the candles she could find and settled down by the fire with a book. The cat sat on the hearthrug at her feet. Because of the height of his hindlegs he always had a little difficulty in arranging his paws. But he did not lie down and fold his paws beneath him for that would have meant a trust he did not feel. The woman noticed this and bent down to stroke him. He jumped on her knees and stayed there.

When the old clock in the hall chimed eleven, the woman blew out all the candles except one. 'Bed,' she said and put a cushion on the hearthrug. But the cat would not lie down

there. He followed her to the door mewing. She hesitated
for a moment and then said: 'Well then, come with me.
You're uneasy tonight.'

With darkness, a wind had sprung up from the south.
Upstairs it sounded more loudly. The dark night outside
seemed like a sea, the house a ship. There were whisperings
and tappings and sighings. Old wood creaked, windows
rattled. The night seemed deeper in the flickering light of
the candle. The dying embers of the turf-fire which the
woman had lit earlier in the evening glimmered among their
ashes. All night long the cat lay with his forepaws across the
woman's legs. He lay there with wide-open eyes, staring at
the dim square of the window. He only moved when his
mistress moved. Sometimes he trembled violently.

The woman lay awake in the darkness. The irregular
whining of the wind, the creaking of the wood, the beating
of the creepers against the window-panes did not disturb
her. But the cat's uneasiness disturbed her. She put out her
hand and stroked him. His soft fur felt cold to the touch.
'There now, go to sleep,' she said. He remained aloof,
suspicious, vigilant.

Then, as she listened, she could hear through the wind and
the creaking small sounds, the gentle slipping of the sea-
gravel on the drive outside; as if someone were padding round
the house. Maybe a stray dog or a fox. The sounds went
away. Then from across the fields she could hear a short,
sharp bark. The cat pressed against her more closely.

Day followed day and the woman's life filled. She came
to know her neighbours. She liked to drop in to the friendly
kitchens and drink a cup of tea. Sometimes she would be
given an egg to take home for her breakfast, a small jug of
cream or a farl of bastable bread. But though she was
received with welcome, the cat was not. Obviously the lack
of a tail rendered him an object of superstitious suspicion.
A belief in witchcraft and the evil eye dies slowly.

The cat soon seemed to have forgotten his first fears.
He frequently went off by himself now. He hunted the
rabbits in the burrows, water-rats on the banks of the river.
He would lie for hours on the branch of a tree and watch
the birds greedily, growling lightly and chattering at them,

dribbling from half open jaws. In the evening he slept on a chair, his paws covering his nose, like a child in prayer. At bedtime he would jump down, suddenly awake, blink and running to the window, demand to be let out.

One day when the woman was working in the garden, the cat came to romp with her. He jumped on her back when she stooped, lay down on the ground, rolled over on his back and begged her to play with him. She stopped work and tickled him with a stick while he clawed the air in ecstasy.

'Your Lordship,' she said, 'You enjoy the fresh earth as much as I do, now don't you? Here under the window I'll plant mignonette and night-scented stock. They don't look much but they smell like heaven. And some nicotina if I can get a root.' She raked over the earth and planted the seed.

That night she was wakened by the cat. He had climbed the wall by the creepers and was mewing hoarsely and insistently outside on the window-sill. She lit the candle and could see his white belly as he stood on his hind-legs and scratched at the panes with his forepaws. She slipped out of bed and raised the lower half of the window. He darted in, rushed across the room and jumped on her bed.

'Poor darling,' she said. 'What is the matter?' He lay close to her as on the first night, trembling and alert. He did not purr when she stroked him but stared hard at the dim outline of the window and growled occasionally.

Night in the country is full of noises. The old house creaked as if with rheumatics. The bushes rustled gently. The creepers tapped incessantly at the window-panes. At a nearby farm a cock crowed. Then in the distance the woman heard a bark.

'A fox,' she murmured. And her hand still caressing the deep fur, she fell asleep.

In the morning she went to look at her work of the day before. She stood looking at it and groaned. Some dog had run hither and thither over it. The seeding would have to be done again and protected by bushes.

When the man came that day with the battery — Mrs. Minihane's this time — she mentioned that a fox had been round the place the night before and had frightened the cat.

'He likely thought him a rabbit,' said the man, his head

on one side.

'I didn't think a fox would come close to a house.'

'It's little ye know them gentry,' laughed the man. 'They'd take the chicken off the kitchen table. Getting very plentiful now we can't get cartridges. And there's no hunt here.'

'Well, I don't like him frightening the cat.'

'Now, ma'am,' the man's voice was low and persuasive. 'Now if you was to have a nice little pom-dog, he'd keep off the fox. I know the one. Very warry he is.'

The woman laughed and shook her head. The man put down the battery on the steps and declined a cup of tea.

'I was wunderin' ma'am, if ye wud like a nice strawberry bed. I've some year-old plants I could spare. I'd come along and fix it up for ye when I bring yer own battery next week.'

'That would be very kind but you must let me pay you.'

'Not a penny, ma'am, thank ye all the same.' His prominent eyes looked fierce with refusal.

'But you must accept something for all your trouble.'

He did not answer for a moment and then said, half-simply, half-cunningly: 'I'm sure, ma'am, if it ever came yer way to do me a kindness, ye wud.'

The woman smiled, almost laughed. It is always so here. Chains of obligation are forced on you.

For a couple of nights the cat kept indoors. Then nature drove him back to his nightly wanderings. The woman propped up the lower half of the window so that he could come in if he wanted. But everything was quiet. He was always there on the door-step in the morning, crying for his milk.

Then one morning he was not there. She went through the garden, through the orchard, down the fields, calling him. But he did not answer. She became alarmed, afraid that he might be caught in a trap. She searched far up the hillside and then the path down the valley to the lake.

She found him not far from the lake. He was dead. She bent and touched the soft fur, smeared with blood, and stroked the cold, stiff, noble head.

'What could have killed him? Who was the enemy?' she cried in tears. She looked around and saw the marks in the soft earth. 'The otter!' she cried. 'It was the otter. Why didn't

I think of it? Oh, my poor darling.'

She wrapped the cat in her scarf and carried him to the house. She placed him on the step and went to fetch the spade.

When she returned the man was there, a basket of plants in one hand, a dog-lead in the other. Beside him stood a light-brown pomeranian dog. The man smiled shyly, his head on one side. 'I brought him for the company. A dog's good company,' he apologized. But the woman was too grieved to notice his little guile. She pointed to the mangled body of the cat. The little man sighed. He put his hand on her arm in sympathy. 'Now don't ye fret,' he said. 'It was to be.' He pushed the lead into her hand. 'Ma'am,' he said, 'take the pom-dog. Else it's the bog-hole for him. The missis won't have him. He chases hens.'

The pomeranian sniffed the air. He was an elderly dog. There was a fine sprinkling of white hairs on his muzzle. The woman let him off the lead and he pranced along the path before her, showing off, with stiff little fore-paws, like a toy soldier. He barked shrilly at nothing and then pranced back.

'Isn't he the fine warry little fella,' said the man wistfully.

The woman sighed. 'It was to be,' she said.

Greater Love

The years were now their enemies. Life had become a hand
casting a glove scarcely worn. Janie and Etta Colgan had
ceased for some time to celebrate or even mention their
birthdays. If, in spite of their wills, they were forced to
realize that they were on such a day a year older, it was to
greet it, like Dean Swift, with prayer and fasting. Days, which
in themselves, seemed so long, rushed after one another with
incredible speed. The clear days of childhood, the fine sweet-
sad evenings of youth now seemed so far away, encased in
their memories like wax flowers under glass.

When Father's grim ferocity had at last been screwed
down in the coffin and covered with white chrysanthemums
— 'How fortunate the greenhouse should be full of them,'
said Etta. 'They would have cost so much to buy.' — it
seemed, to Etta, that the lid of the box in which they had
always lived, had at last been raised. Now they could stretch
their cramping limbs in the sunshine of life.

Mr. Wilson, their solicitor, called after the funeral, and, in
the still darkened dining-room, read their father's will. They
were rich women, a fact which surprised them. Father, it
seemed, had made a fortune building the wretched one-
eyed hovels which housed the mill-hands, and then by careful
speculation had increased it. Yet since their earliest
childhood Father had been careful to raise them with the
spectre of poverty always before their eyes. He curbed even
the slightest extravagance. Now there was no longer any need
to cover the table-cloth with newspapers during meals, or
change only one sheet at a time on their bed. They need no

longer wear cobbled shoes or turned skirts. They could even
keep a little dog. Etta had always wanted a little dog to take
for walks. Janie, suddenly realizing these things, too, burst
into tears. Mr. Wilson and Etta rushed to her side.

'Forgive me,' she sobbed. 'But all that money. What will
we do with it?'

'Don't worry about that, my dear,' said Mr. Wilson and
patted her back. 'The trustees will look after it for you. Just
spend the income and see you enjoy it.'

If Etta thought life would be different, she was mistaken.
Janie was too deeply sunk in petty economies to abandon
them. She did, however, yield to her younger sister on certain
points. The mortifying newspapers were a thing of the past,
both sheets were changed each week. They had a holiday in
Portrush. But there it had ended. The holiday had been a
failure. They had not enjoyed spending money. They could
not play games nor go swimming. The people at the hotel, so
smart and self-assured, terrified them. They were glad to be
home again. And Janie refused to let Etta have a little dog.
She saw no sense, she said, in feeding an animal for nothing.

The economy to which Father had accustomed them had
led to complete social isolation. They neither entertained
nor were asked anywhere. Their home, a square box of a
house with bay windows and heavy lace curtains, stood at
the corner of the Workhouse Road where building lots had
been cheap because of the grim stone wall which con-
fronted them, built in the bad years, to close away from sight
the poor and miserable, too old or too weak to work in the
mills. After the funeral their doctor and his wife called and
urged them to come visiting. And the Methodist minister and
his wife came to invite them to all the church functions. But
they continued as before. They went to the library twice a
week to change their books. Every afternoon they went
walking and in the evening they read and played duets on the
piano. Janie did all the cooking and Etta was a wonderful
gardener.

She had turned the old builder's yard at the back and the
side of the house into a paved walk and garden. It was quite
a show place, even handsomer than Mrs. Wilmore's garden
where two gardeners were kept. It was Etta's boast that all

the year round she had flowers.

And Janie, as she baked her pies and made chocolate layer cake for Sunday tea or while stirring the red gooseberry jam, delicately flavoured with elder flowers, often smiled as she looked out through the kitchen window to see her sister's stern in the air, for all the world like a duck in a pond, and the two stout legs in brown lisle stockings, with the fringe of pink knickers showing, looked as if they grew out of the earth she handled with such loving care. Then, suddenly, Etta would straighten her back and brush back the curling tendrils of faded, fair hair with her wrist from her small-featured pink face. She was a short, sturdy woman who had never, even in her youth, had any pretension to beauty.

It was Janie who had been pretty. It was Janie who noticed the marks left by those years they no longer counted. Janie sighed when she saw the grey hair creep through her light brown head and the crow's feet around Etta's eyes. Etta, who had never expected much from life, had a more contented spirit.

One Saturday afternoon, when she had taken the bread from the oven and put in the cakes, Janie sauntered out to the garden to watch her sister. Etta was tidying a border.

'It should look very fine this year,' said Etta. 'It's to be a white border. An edging of white violas, with pinks and dwarf snapdragon behind. Then against the grey wall, phlox and white gladiolas and over there,' she pointed with her hoe, 'just near that old corner where they used to mix the mortar, are St. Joseph's lilies. They love old mortar.'

'I don't much care for white flowers,' said Janie. 'They put me in mind of funerals.'

'Well, they put me in mind of weddings,' said Etta, cheerfully. 'You'll like it when you see it.'

'Tomorrow the new minister is to preach,' said Janie.

'So he is,' said Etta, her head on one side as she continued to look at the border.

'I was wondering,' said Janie, 'Ought we to wear our new best?'

It was their custom to keep their new clothes in the wardrobe for at least six months before wearing them. Just to get themselves accustomed to the idea of their newness.

'Well, we might,' said Etta. 'It's an occasion. They wouldn't be noticed so much.'

'I was wondering about the shoes. They don't look too remarkable, do they, with those open straps?'

'No, Janie, you've got a very neat foot. You might as well show it off. We can go the whole hog in honour of the new minister. Clothes are only new once.'

They set off early the next morning, partly because the new shoes irked slightly, partly to be in their pew before most of the congregation and so avoid the awkwardness of walking down the aisle with their new clothes on. The chapel had been built by Father and he had selected the pew beneath the pulpit for himself because he was getting a little deaf. They had plenty of time to settle themselves comfortably and Janie was able to unfasten the strap of the shoe which pinched before the service began.

From first to last, Janie and Etta could hardly take their eyes off the new minister. He was a tall, delicate-looking young man, with a very pink and white complexion, large pale-blue eyes and fair hair which was already receding from a high forehead. His actions were devout without a shade of ritualism. His voice was clear and deep. During the sermon he leaned forward over the pulpit and addressed the congregation in an intimate and brotherly manner. Janie and Etta forgot the embarrassment of their new clothes. Janie even forgot the pinching shoes. They were thrilled. Their heads leaned towards one another as they listened, drinking in every word. And every word seemed addressed to them.

The following Wednesday, Janie and Etta took the weekly excursion train to Belfast. They were going, ostensibly, to buy new curtains for the drawing-room. At least that is what they talked about in the railway carriage. But when they arrived at Victoria Station, they hurried through the streets, as if to get away as quickly as possible from their fellow-travellers and made their way to a large hair-dressing establishment. There they each had a beauty treatment, a facial massage, a manicure and most daring, their hair brightened and set. Not dyed — the young lady assured them — just brightened. Then, blushing with embarrassment, they rushed to a large department store and bought some curtain material. Etta recovered more quickly than her sister from this upheaval, enough at any rate to have an argument with the assistant about the quality of the material he showed them. Janie sat in a chair almost incapable of speech and watched Etta with admiration as the suddenly 'brightened' head bent over the counter and her sister declared: 'Curtains are not bought every day. Show me something will wear.' And turning to Janie she added, 'I'd like to have the new curtains up before Mr. Wallace calls.'

Just as if she had never any thought in her mind but curtains.

Mr. Wallace was not long in calling. As the most wealthy pew-holders, their names were at the head of the list the outgoing minister had left him. He sat on a low stool and looked up at them, first at Etta, then at Janie, with large enquiring eyes. His conversation was of the lightly facetious order favoured by clergymen when they call on ladies, a mixture of parish chatter and safe, simple jokes. He devoured Janie's chocolate cake while complimenting her on its excellence. He listened in wrapt admiration to a duet and even suggested coming round of an evening to practice some songs if the ladies would be so kind as to play his accompaniments.

'And do you like this part of the country, Mr. Wallace?' Janie asked.

'Very much indeed. Charming country, and the town is beautifully situated. There must be some lovely walks around.'

'My sister and I enjoy the river walk. When the weather is fine we go there almost every day. There's a path along the bank and the trees make fine shade,' said Etta.

Janie blushed for her younger sister and hoped Mr. Wallace would not think her too forward. It sounded just as if she were dropping a hint. She added hastily: 'Oh no, Etta dear. Not every day. Only on *very* fine days. The path gets so muddy in the rain.'

But Mr. Wallace did not seem to notice Etta's forwardness. He smiled up at Janie and said: 'I shall probably run into you there some day soon.'

And so he did. For the very next day when Janie and Etta

stepped that way, he came to meet them. He fell into step beside them and conversed easily about the weather, the landscape, other landscapes, his former curacy in the city, his work. He was a man who made conversation without effort, suiting it unconsciously to the ears of his listeners. When he arrived at their gate and took off his hat to wish them goodbye, Etta said: 'Do come in, Mr. Wallace and take tea with us. Janie has baked another chocolate cake.'

'Delighted,' he said and followed them in.

Very soon he was a regular caller. And it seemed as if with the passing days the sisters grew younger. The fine lines around their eyes only showed now when they laughed. Their step became lighter, the lines of their bodies lost stiffness and flowed. Mr. Wallace seemed very happy in their company. He sang duets with Janie and played chess with Etta who was sometimes tactless enough, so Janie thought, to beat him. Then one day he came to wish them goodbye. He was going away for a holiday.

'Oh dear, we shall miss you. Won't we, Etta?' said Janie.

'Indeed we will,' said Etta. 'And where are you going, Mr. Wallace? Home?'

'Ah no,' he said sadly. 'I have no home since my dear mother died.'

'I'm so sorry,' said Janie and Etta together.

'Yes, indeed. And since her death this is the first place which has given me any feeling of home. You've no idea how much your house has come to mean to me.'

Janie and Etta murmured, 'We're so glad.'

'I've come to make a request which I hope you will grant. May I write to you while I am away?'

Janie looked at Etta and Etta looked at Janie. Then both looked at Mr. Wallace and nodded.

'Of course,' they said. 'Why not?'

For the first time in their lives, Janie and Etta waited with beating hearts for the postman. When he passed their gate, they turned sadly away from the curtains behind which they were hiding. If he dropped a circular or bill into the letter-box, their disappointment was even greater. Then one day, a week after Mr. Wallace's departure, the letter came. It was addressed to Janie in a large, flowing handwriting. Etta stood beside her impatiently while she opened it.

Janie held the letter away from her because she was getting a trifle long-sighted. She read the first two lines, then went very red and then white. She sat down abruptly on a chair and began to tremble. She pressed one hand to her mouth, the other with the letter to her breast.

'Janie, Janie, what's the matter?' cried Etta. 'Is it bad news?' And she put out her hand for the letter.

'It's a proposal,' said Janie feebly.

Etta laughed with delight.

'And what's that to get upset about? I was expecting it.'

'But, Etta, why me? I thought it was you he liked. You and he got on so well together.'

'It only goes to show he has some sense,' said Etta.

'But you're much younger.'

'Not much, Janie. A year or two makes no difference. You're by far the prettier. I'm as plain as a loaf, always was.'

'You're not disappointed, Etta?'

Etta laughed. 'Disappointed? Good gracious, no. If ever I marry, it will be an old grand-daddy, who'll make a pet of me, like you do.'

The strain on Janie's face was vanishing. She was beginning to laugh and cry at the same time, bewildered. 'What a funny girl you are, Etta. What will I answer?'

'Why, "yes", of course.'

'But how? How?'

'With pen and paper,' Etta teased.

But it was not so easy. Janie sat down at the table to compose the letter with Etta by her side.

'How ought I to begin?' she asked.

' "My dear Jim," ' said Etta.

'No, dear. I couldn't. Yet Mr. Wallace sounds so formal.'

'Well, what about "Dear James", then?'

So 'Dear James' it was.

It took them the whole morning, and a great deal of spoiled paper to write the answer. When it was finished, Etta had to take it out of Janie's hand because she was still unsatisfied with the phrasing.

'Glory be!' she said. 'Anybody would think it was easy to write, "Dear James, wedding bells, with all my heart." And here you are worrying over every word.' So without waiting for her sister to call back the letter, she put on her hat and carried it to the post.

The answer came back before they expected it, in the form of a telegram. Etta opened it, because telegrams were regarded as things of ill omen in this house. She handed it to her sister with a smile. It read: 'Proverbs 31, ten and eleven. Love, James.'

'Well, he hasn't exceeded the twelve words,' said Etta.

They rushed together to the drawing-room where Father's Bible lay on the small table by the window. Etta turned the pages quickly and then read aloud: 'Who can find a virtuous woman? for her price is above rubies. The heart of her husband doth safely trust in her, so that he shall have no need of spoil.'

'How lovely!' said Janie softly. 'I'll have it engraved on my wedding ring. Proverbs 31, ten and eleven.'

'Didn't I tell you, Janie, when I made the white border, it was for a wedding?' said Etta.

'When do you think he'll be back?' said Janie.

'Very soon, I expect.'

'How can I meet him? I am so nervous.'

'Nonsense! Think how nice it will be when it's over. Like the dentist.'

James returned the following day. Etta opened the door to him with a smile of welcome and then pointing to the drawing-room door, went away.

During the following weeks it was Etta who arranged everything. With the help of the daily charwoman, she moved furniture and rearranged rooms, for it was decided that James should come to live with them. The residence attached to the church was dark and small and had no garden. It was Etta who bought the trousseau, saw the caterers and decorated the church with her own flowers. Janie went through those weeks as if in a dream.

Etta thought the wedding the most beautiful ceremony she had ever seen. She could scarcely take her eyes from her sister's face. She thought Janie had never looked so lovely, not even years ago when they were both young and fancied themselves in love with the new doctor who passed their gate on his way to the workhouse hospital. She smiled to herself as she remembered and wondered if Janie ever thought of those days now when that same doctor, grown bald and corpulent, came to see her. And did she now recall those days of despair when he came back from Dublin with a young wife who sat now plump and elderly beside her husband, while Janie, lovely Janie, stood tall and slim and beautiful, if a little tired-looking, beside a young and handsome husband. Etta suddenly felt so much older than her sister, so much wiser. For she had no beauty to call back. As she looked at Janie, she had all the feelings of a mother who watches an only daughter launched on the world, the same longing to protect, the same agony of apprehension, the same pride in her triumph.

And even after the simple wedding breakfast, when the newly married couple had gone off to London to spend their honeymoon there, Etta was busy. She had the task of furnishing the morning-room as a study for her brother-in-law, carpenters to oversee, furniture to buy. It was a very pleasant room when it was ready, though it smelled rather of fresh paint. She thought of the splendid sermons he would write there.

When Janie and her husband returned Etta looked sharply at her sister's face. Janie looked radiant. She was full of chatter about all she had seen. Etta had a fine supper ready for them. James ate a lot and seemed rather absent-minded, scarcely adding a word to the conversation, except when directly spoken to.

After supper he retired to his study to work on his sermon for the next day, and the two sisters drew up to the fire with their books, just as if nothing had happened to change their lives. Etta sat with her feet on the fender, her book held between her face and the fire, warming her shins. Janie reclined in her armchair. Presently she turned her book face downward on her knees and said:

'Etta dear, I want to say something to you. Something important.'

'Well, my dear, what is it?' And Etta's heart missed a beat. Her sister's voice sounded so serious.

'It's about money, Etta. We have so much money, more

than we can ever use. And James has so little. I know it irks
him, makes him feel, well, inferior. He doesn't like me to pay
the bills. And how can he afford to? There are so many
calls on a clergyman's purse. I've been thinking. Couldn't
we have some money made over to him?'

Etta frowned. Was this the meaning of her brother-in-
law's distant manner at supper. Was it possible he had been
bullying Janie? She was up in arms to defend her sister, even
against that sister's wish.

'I should have thought he had enough. He has no household expenses here.'

'But, Etta, you must understand, he has a place in the
world. And he wants to do so much for the poor of his parish
and the young people. His income is pitiably small.'

Etta continued to frown at the fire. She did not dare to
look at Janie. She must not weaken.

'Your money's your own. It has nothing to do with me,'
she said abruptly.

'But it has, Etta. You know the money is held in trust for
both of us, the survivor to inherit all, if there are no
children.'

'Well, it's too soon to be thinking of that. All I say, is,
make him what allowance you wish. But no capital.'

'He won't like that, Etta.'

'He must. I'll not give my consent to any capital changing
hands. But you can go and see Mr. Wilson.'

'Oh, Etta,' said Janie. 'I thought you loved me.'

But Etta did not weaken. If Janie's hold over her husband
was her money, then Janie was not going to part with that
money.

'I do, my dear,' she said. 'But I'm not a fool about James
Wallace. Now Janie, don't cry. I like the man well enough.
I'll agree to what Mr. Wilson says.'

Mr. Wilson agreed with Etta.

James Wallace, aware, perhaps, of his sister-in-law's cool
and far-seeing eyes, professed himself well content with the
additional income of five hundred pounds which the trustees
unwillingly agreed to pay him. He became once again his old,
amiable, smiling self, singing duets with his wife in the
evening to Etta's accompaniment, walking with them when

they took a stroll by the river in the afternoon, and seeing
them off on the train when they went to Belfast to have
their hair brightened. Etta would have given up her fight
against time, but she felt she could not desert her sister.

The days began again to slip evenly away, through autumn
and winter and then, before they realized it, spring was on
them and Etta was busy in the garden. Janie still did the
cooking and helped her husband with parish work. Then Etta
began to notice something. Her brother-in-law began to go
away by himself from time to time.

'It's just a meeting of clergy to discuss youth problems,
my dear. You'd be bored alone all day in the hotel,' he
explained to his wife.

And Janie, simple and loving, had agreed. But Etta was not
so easily deceived. One day, when turning out the study, she
pulled a suitcase down from the top of a cupboard, where it
lay concealed. She opened it and found a tweed suit, a hat
and two soft shirts. One of the shirts needed laundering. She
closed the case, put it back and said nothing to Janie. She
waited and watched. The next time James Wallace made the
usual excuse to go away, this time more casually than before,
she followed him into the study and pointing to where the
suitcase lay, said: 'I'm no fool, James, even if Janie is. Do
you want me to tell her what you've hidden in that suitcase? Do you want her to know you are a liar and a
deceiver?'

He turned on her viciously. Etta was quite appalled at the
change which came over him.

'You spy!' he hissed. 'Trying to make trouble between
man and wife. I know you. I know your mean, jealous
nature. For two pins I'd take Janie out of this and never let
you see her again.'

There was such force of vindictive malice in his face that
Etta realized that what she had first thought was weakness
was in reality wickedness. And more than ever she felt her
sister's need for protection and left the room without a word.
Her one anxiety now was to prevent Janie finding out the
true nature of her husband. She became quiet and affable.
She agreed with every word James Wallace said and flattered
him in the presence of her sister. She let him think she feared

him. When his absences from home became more frequent,
it was she who forestalled his excuses. She even said one day
to Janie: 'There now, Janie, be sensible. Men weary of
women's company and like to get away with other men.'

'Even from a wife, Etta?'

'Even from a nice wife like you. They want to talk about
their own affairs. Cheer up, girl, he'll be home tomorrow.'

But even the most watchful eyes cannot foresee
everything. One day when James was away and Etta busy in
the garden, she heard a cry. She rushed indoors. Janie was
standing beside her husband's desk, a sheet of paper in her
hand. Her head shook like the head of one of those dolls on
wires, which bob and tremble when touched. She held out
the paper to Etta. 'I was reading his sermon,' she said in a
choking voice. 'His sermon. It was beautiful and then — I
found — this.'

Etta glanced at the page. She had already guessed what it
was. A letter, a love letter, written to make an appointment
and it had slipped between the pages of the sermon. She
dropped the page on the floor and turning to her sister, took
her in her arms. The two heads leaned together, two dyed
heads. Two middle-aged women wept in one another's arms.

It was Etta who recovered first.

'Sit down, Janie. Sit down, dear,' she said and waited until
she thought Janie had recovered from the first shock. She
dried her own eyes and tucked the handkerchief firmly into
her belt. She picked up the letter and placed it between the
pages of the sermon. Then turning to her sister she spoke
slowly and calmly as to a frightened child.

'Janie dear, it's terrible, I know. But there's something
you must promise me. You must be wise. You won't say a
word about this to James.'

'But, Etta, I must, I must. How could I go on?' And
her voice rose shrilly in another burst of hysteria.

'You must try to go on — to go on as if nothing had
happened.'

'I can't. I can't,' wailed Janie. 'It will kill me. It will kill
me.'

'It won't. You've got to be sensible. Other wives learn and
so must you. So long as he hides things, all is not lost. It

means he still cares for you. Don't you see? You must behave, normally. He must suspect nothing. I expect most men are the same and most wives learn to be silent.'

'James isn't most men. He's a clergyman.'

'I tell you it makes no difference, Janie. They're all the same. If you want to lose him altogether, then let him know. If you want him to stay, keep your counsel.'

When James Wallace returned, Etta met him in the hall. 'Janie hasn't been well,' she said quietly. 'Nothing but a nasty turn of migraine. She will be better tomorrow. I've put her in my room for quiet.'

And so Janie's pale and strained face was excused when she came downstairs the next day.

'What you need is fresh air, my dear,' said her husband. 'We'll go for a walk this afternoon.'

'Yes, Janie,' said Etta. 'We'll go for a walk by the river. It's a lovely day.'

It was a lovely day. The air was warm with the promise of summer. Small white clouds trundled across the blue sky on a light breeze. The crab apple trees along the banks of the river were pink and white with blossom, and everywhere in the bushes the birds sang sweetly. Across the hill came the clear notes of the cuckoo. James was in pleasant humour, took his wife's arm and chatted pleasantly. Etta began to gather a large bunch of wild flowers. She ran here and there, laughing and talking as she went. 'Look, Janie, at the water-hen.' Or, 'See, Janie, what a lot of crab apples we'll have this year for the jelly. Do you like apple jelly, James? You must like Janie's. It's wonderful. She flavours it with the scented geranium.'

Suddenly she stopped by the river bank to pick another flower and looking down into the water, said suddenly and seriously: 'James, come here. No, not you, Janie.'

'What is it?' he asked.

'Come here and see. Something in the water.' Her voice sounded low and nervous.

He left his wife and came forward. He bent over the running stream. Then Janie saw her sister stand up straight and throw her flowers away. With all her force, and Etta was strong, she pushed James Wallace. He tottered for a moment and then, half turning, made a grab and caught Etta's skirt. Then Etta, without one moment's hesitation, hurled herself and her brother-in-law into the deep, murky stream. Janie, unable to move, screamed. She screamed when she saw James appear again on the surface, and screamed again when she saw her sister's hand seize him by the collar and drag him down, down. Then two men came running across the fields. And a woman came and took her away.

The whole town came to the funeral, stirred to the depths by the story of the young clergyman who had drowned in an attempt to save his sister-in-law's life. A colleague from a neighbourhood parish said a few words at the grave-side. 'Greater love,' he said, 'hath no man.' And Janie, standing beside him, in a cheap black coat and hat, thought only of her sister. She could never put away from her the memory of her sister's hand as it seized her husband and dragged him under. 'Greater love hath no man,' she thought. Not only to give her life, but her place in Heaven, her hope of eternity. Greater love hath no man.

She went back to the lonely house. It was very quiet there behind the drawn blinds. She covered the tablecloth with a newspaper and made herself a cup of tea.

Original Sin

Every Sunday morning after breakfast my cousin Justin and I found our prayer books and set out for Sunday School. Here, in the bare Church of Ireland schoolroom the Reverend James Mortimer instructed us and the other Protestant children of the parish in the catechism, the scriptures and the meaning of the ritual. We learned a great deal, even if we understood very little. We repeated by heart the collect for the day, a couple of verses of a psalm, a verse of a hymn and answered to the best of our ability a certain number of set questions. If we did well and made few mistakes we were presented at the end of the lesson with a small coloured text with a number written on the back. When we had ten of these we could exchange them for a larger one and when we had five large ones we could exchange these for a large illuminated text suitable for framing and putting over the bed.

We did not like Mr. Mortimer. We suspected him of meanness. He often withheld a text which we felt was merited. He had neither charm of person nor manner, a thin little man with a pointed nose and shortsighted eyes. He wore pincenez. He walked in a peculiar rocking manner so that we were sure that he had wooden feet. He was exact over trifles and very much resented being questioned. While despising the papal authority himself, he was more dictatorial in matter of doctrine than any pope. We were accustomed to asking our Grandfather questions and getting intelligent answers. Mr. Mortimer did not descend to our level. He presented us with irrefutable doctrine.

Justin who was older than I by about three years and having an inquiring turn of mind, asked many questions. What was a cubit? How much was a sheckel? What was baptism? Why did it wash away your sins when you were only a few days old and had none? What was original sin? Mr. Mortimer's replies were the usual stereotyped ones. He scorned explanation. If pushed for further information he would say that Justin had not been paying attention to the lessons and withheld the small text.

This we took badly. We had set our hearts on presenting Aunt Molly with two large illuminated texts on her birthday. We were sure she would have them framed and put up over her bed. Aunt Molly, who knew nothing of the bribe system of instruction Mr. Mortimer had introduced, noticed our interest in the little texts. The next time she went to Derry she brought us back a couple of envelopes full of them. We immediately formed the brilliant plan of numbering them ourselves and presenting them the following Sunday, a hundred of them, to be exchanged for two large illuminated holy pictures.

Children are always astonished when they find that grown up people understand their subterfuges. Our astonishment was turned to indignation when we were held up in front of the other children as liars and cheats. We felt that we had not deserved this. Even if Mr. Mortimer were the nearest thing on earth to God, this gave him no right to cover us with shame and ignominy. After all we had handed in genuine small texts, even if we had not earned them. Hadn't Mr. Mortimer himself said that he would give us one large text in exchange for ten small ones and the illuminated picture text for five large texts? And hadn't we given him fifty each? Couldn't the man count? Hadn't we numbered them?

We left Sunday School crestfallen and miserable. But we soon recovered and lost all interests in texts. We gave Aunt Molly a bar of chocolate and a jewelled pin costing sixpence for her birthday and were comforted by her assurance that that was just what she had been longing for.

Wet days were always difficult days. When we had finished our lessons and fed the dogs, there was very little to do. Sometimes Aunt Molly would find us a job or a book to read.

Sometimes she told us to go and play. We would wander round the house, looking out through one window after another and wishing the rain would stop. Sometimes we would go to the dark room and root around for old clothes to dress up in.

The dark room opened off the gun room and it had no window. It was the mysterious storeroom of all the cast off rubbish of the ages. Here everything that was not wanted was stored; old furniture, old clothes, old trunks, old carpets, odds and ends of china, schoolbooks long out of date, broken fishing rods, and a cottage piano. We would light the storm lantern and spend hours there searching. One day we made an amazing discovery. We found a collection of silver coins. If it had rained silver from heaven, we could not have been more surprised and delighted. We took one which looked like a rather large shilling, and putting on our waterproofs, sneaked out and made a tour of the village shops, to try and turn it into sweets. But no one would accept it as legal tender. We sat down and wondered what we could do about it.

'I tell you what,' said Justin. 'We'll try it on the collection on Sunday.'

'Oh, Justin, we daren't' I said. 'What would Mr. Mortimer say?'

'How would he know?' said Justin. 'It might have been anybody who put it on. It might be Mr. MacGuiness or Dr. Hare or Mrs. Starrett.'

'Wouldn't God know?' I said.

'He won't say anything,' said Justin.

Every week we got twopence pocket money and every Sunday morning Grandfather gave us a shilling each for our collection money. It was useless to try and put the pennies on the plate and keep the shilling. Ours was the first pew and the pennies would be noticed. It was possible, however, that these coins might escape detection. We spent a happy afternoon polishing them up.

The following Sunday we tried it. My courage almost gave way at the last moment but greed triumphed in the end and I followed Justin's example and placed my coin beside his. Neither Grandfather nor Aunt Molly noticed anything amiss. We hoped that Mr. Mortimer was equally blind. We spent an anxious week, half expecting to be denounced in church the following Sunday as liars and cheats. But nothing happened, so we plucked up our courage and began again. This lasted for several weeks. We squandered our shillings on sweets of all sorts from liquorice laces to boxes of chocolates and though Aunt Molly was sometimes vaguely apprehensive about our slight loss of appetite, our digestion stood up to the strain very well. But all things come to an end and after some time we were back on our twopenny allowance again and in time forgot all about the mysterious silver coins.

From time to time we were invited with Aunt Molly to tea at the Rectory. We always hoped to escape this treat but in vain. We never caught cold just at the right time nor developed any infectious symptoms. We always said we didn't feel well and couldn't eat any dinner thank you, but when it was put on our plates we had not the self-control to abstain.

These visits were dull affairs. Mrs. Mortimer, a nosy woman whom we suspected of wearing a wig, would meet us and walk us round the garden. We were carefully warned at every step to avoid treading on anything but the path. The yard was totally devoid of livestock. The Mortimers kept no pets. There wasn't even a great deal to eat and what there was was very dull, bread and butter, rock buns and a small slice of fruit cake. We had to wear our best clothes and sit on stiff chairs. Our only amusement was looking at pictures of the Holy Land through the spectroscope. The minutes dragged slowly on until the blessed one arrived when we could run screaming down the road home in front of Aunt Molly.

This time there was a slight variation. No sooner had we made the round of the garden and entered the drawing room than Mrs. Mortimer drew Aunt Mollie's attention to a small glass case. Inside the case, mounted on velvet were the coins we had passed on to the collection plate.

'My husband's latest hobby,' she said. 'He is collecting coins now. Much more interesting than postage stamps, I think.'

'Indeed,' said Aunt Molly, 'Most interesting. My father

used to collect coins. I wonder where they are now? Somewhere about, I suppose.'

'Perhaps the children would like to see them?' said Mrs.
Mortimer. 'Look Louise, look Justin. There is a Queen Anne
shilling. Interesting, isn't it. Queen Anne died such a long
time ago, oh, more than a hundred years, I suppose.

We looked, our eyes nearly dropping out with horror. Next
would come exposure and shame. We were about to be
branded as liars and cheats in front of Aunt Molly. All this
had been a carefully worked up plot. The blood rushed to
our faces. Denial never even entered our minds. We felt like
cornered rabbits, sitting quiet in the face of the inevitable.
We did not dare to look at one another.

But we could not stand there like idiots staring at the
coins for ever. When we did look up a strange sight met our
eyes. Not a Mr. Mortimer filled with righteous wrath, but an
uncomfortable elderly clergyman shuffling on what we were
so sure were his wooden feet and twirling his pince-nez with
nervous fingers. His face was flushed. His naked eyes looked
worried. We slowly came to our senses. Our fear melted away
and an unnatural jubilation took its place. We knew that he
knew that we knew. And in this knowledge we graciously
forgave.

The Pedlar and the Lady

It was raining heavily, steadily. Grey clouds, which hung like curtains from the sky, drifted cumberously before the south-west wind, obscuring the landscape. All that could be seen was the whitish road, bordered by stone walls, fading into the distance. Water ran in rivulets along it, making it like the bed of a shallow stream. Nothing could be heard but the whistling of the wind, the singing of the telegraph poles, the occasional cough of a sheltering sheep, the cry of a curlew.

There was no sign of human habitation.

A hawker struggled along the road, his head bent low against the storm. He wore an old fur cap pulled down over his ears. It made his head look like that of a dog just out of the water. He was enveloped in a huge Inverness coat, which covered him almost to his feet. Around his throat and mouth he had wound a long woollen scarf. From time to time he halted, grunting, and shifted the heavy pack into another position on his shoulders.

Suddenly out of the rain and mist, there appeared on the right hand side of the road a great stone barn. On the sheltered side of it stood a large hay-rick. The hawker stopped, looked at it for a few seconds and then at the wet road before him. Grunting he passed through a gap in the loose stone wall. One side of the barn door was open. He approached timorously, hesitatingly, as if he feared he was transgressing some law.

It was dark inside the barn. The hawker stood blinking in the doorway, trying to penetrate the gloom. Presently he saw hay piled up at the far end, a heap of turnips just inside the door, and half blocking the entrance, a farm cart. He turned his back on all this and looked out again on the dreary landscape. The light was beginning to fade, the rain was falling more heavily than ever. There was no sign of the wind shifting. It would rain until near dawn. Then the wind might veer a point and the sky clear. It was a good five Irish miles to the nearest village, and the farmhouses were far away from the road. With a weary sigh he turned again and moved towards the hay.

Something moved at the back of the barn. He stopped short, peering through the darkness. He saw the glint of a revolver in a white hand.

'Halt!' came a hard, low voice, 'Stay where you are or I'll fire. Who are you?'

The hawker started and uttered a cry like a hunted rabbit. He seemed incapable of speech. Instead he waved his hands frantically above his head.

'Who are you?' asked the voice again in a harsh, insistent tone, 'What are you doing here?'

'Nothing, nothing, indeed nothing!' answered the hawker in a soft foreign accent, the words now tumbling out of his mouth, his hands still gesticulating wildly. 'I am a pedlar. The rain is very heavy and I saw this shelter. It's five miles to the village and not a house on the way. I thought no one would mind if I stayed here till morning. I won't do no harm, just sleep here till the storm is over. I don't smoke. I won't strike matches. I'll not hurt anything if I can just sleep here in the hay.'

There was a murmur of voices and the hawker realized there was more than one person present. He became even more frightened.

'If you like I will go away,' he said, turning towards the door.

'No, no, you won't!' the voice almost shouted. 'Now you're here you'll damn well stay here. I'm not going to let you down to the village to tell everyone we're here. You can stay and keep quiet until we leave. Come in here to the back so that we can see you. You've no gun, have you, no stick?'

'I've never had a gun in my life,' replied the hawker nervously, stretching out both hands. 'They frighten me.

What would I do with a gun? See, no gun, no stick, nothing!'

'Come back here then,' commanded the man in the hay,
'but drop your pack there first.'

The hawker let his pack fall to the ground and advanced.
His eyes were now accustomed to the obscurity. He saw two
figures leaning up against the pile of hay; one tall and heavy,
the other small and slight. Both had revolvers.

He leant up against the hay beside them, embarrassed and
terrified. He hardly dared glance at them. They whispered
together. Suddenly the smaller figure turned towards him
and asked: 'Have you met anyone on the road?'

He started again and threw out his hands as if protecting
himself. The voice was the voice of a woman, of a well-bred
gentlewoman at that. She was dressed in a long coat, a tweed
hat pulled down over her ears, and top boots. He had thought
she was a boy.

'No, ma'am, no,' he replied, gaping at her, 'No one at all.'

'You're very wet,' she said. 'You'd better bury yourself
in the hay. You'll get warm that way. Otherwise you'll catch
cold, get very ill.'

The hawker began to make a hole for himself in the hay.
But as he was about to step into it, he hesitated.

'I beg your pardon, ma'am,' he asked, 'but would you not
get into the hay. The night is cold and I am sure you're wet
too.'

'Do, Eleanor,' said the man, 'We won't leave here until the
storm passes and that won't be before tomorrow morning.
Get some sleep. I'll watch.'

The hawker felt happier now and safer. He busied himself
with the hay. He covered the woman up carefully, gently
removing stray straws which might tickle her face.

'If you would like a nice clean handkerchief from my
pack, ma'am, to put under your head, it would keep the hay
away and you would sleep more comfortably.'

'You are very kind,' she murmured, when the hawker
returned with a large, red, cotton handkerchief, which he
placed gently under her head. 'Where do you come from?
You're a stranger here. What is your name?'

'My name is Joseph Stein, but hereabouts they call me Joe
Pedlar. My brother and I, we have a small draper's shop in

Fountain Street, Derry. He looks after the shop and I go peddling. Oh, I'm well known through the country. I sell small things and take orders from the farmers' wives. They like me. They think I have very good taste. I know what they like. I always send them good, solid stuff for they don't like the light flimsy garments the factory girls wear in the city. Value, I give value.'

'But you were not born there. I know Derry. I live there. You must have been born in another country. You have a foreign accent.'

'Yes, yes, I was born in Russia. Then when there came trouble and fighting, I left. I came first to Hull and then to Glasgow, and then when I made a little money, I moved over to Derry. There were better opportunities of making a business.'

'Why did you leave Russia? I could not live anywhere but here where I was born.'

'Because of the persecutions. Often have we sat trembling in our houses, or praying in the Schul, waiting for the terrible moment when the Cossacks would ride through the town, killing, raping, burning. But that was not the worst. Violent fury passes. When my son was born, I was frightened. I did not want him to grow up and be taken away and made a soldier.'

'Yes, I have heard that terrible things happen in Russia,' the woman sighed. 'They happen everywhere. Is your family with you in Derry?'

'They are all with me at last in my little house in Fountain Street. When business is better, then we will buy a better house, in a nicer part of the town. The children are going to school. They are clever. They are making progress. But if I might ask, ma'am, what is your name? Where do you live?'

'My home is in Derry too, on the other side of the town, you know, the Waterside, beyond the Barracks, near the sea. But I do not live there very much. I am always with my husband. I am surprised that you do not know my name. You must have heard it often enough in the farmhouses. It is Eleanor Spain.'

'Spain!' cried the hawker, 'Spain, the agent!'

'Aye,' growled the man, turning quickly round, 'Spain,

the land agent, Lord Carramore's agent. And if those dirty
swine of farmers think they can frighten me, they're
mistaken. They pay their rent or out they go into the ditch.'

The hawker felt the woman's hand steal over his mouth to
prevent him speaking. But he was too frightened to speak.
He just lay back in the hay, trembling. The agent took a
step away from the stack as if to go towards the door, then
stopped and turned round.

'They're waiting in the village for me, aren't they, Pedlar?
They think they have me now, trapped like a weasel in a
hole. They'll plant a bullet in my back, kill me like a dog!
That's what you've heard, Pedlar, isn't it? But they are
mistaken. I'll outwit them yet, the cowardly curs.'

He strode to the door and stood there looking out into
the night. For some time no one spoke in the barn. There was
no sound except the howling of the storm. The hawker
thought that surely everyone could hear the beating of his
heart. He sighed heavily to relieve the congestion of fear. He
moved nearer the woman as if she were his protector.
Presently Eleanor Spain extricated herself from the nest
of hay and followed her husband to the door. She stood
there beside him for some minutes without speaking. Then a
conversation began in low tones. The hawker strained his
ears in the darkness. But all he could hear was the word
'police', repeated several times. He trembled more than ever

Then Eleanor Spain came back to her place in the hay,
leaving her husband at the door. For a little while she said
nothing, keeping very still in her nest. The hawker was too
frightened to begin a conversation. Suddenly she turned to
him and said:

'You are very friendly with the peasants of the neighbourhood, aren't you?'

'Yes, ma'am. They are very kind to me, a stranger. They
ask me into their houses and offer me food. I bring round
the paper with me and tell them bits of news. I bring
messages from one farm to another. Believe me, ma'am, they
are kind, decent people.'

'It is hard to know that when you are in our position. I
realize that they have their grievances, serious ones. But I
cannot be expected to sympathize with them when I know

they may put a bullet into my husband at any moment.
But I don't want to talk about rights and wrongs. Women
have little interest in these matters, you know. I want you to
do me a favour. Will you?'

'Of course, ma'am, if I can.'

'We wondered, my husband and I, if you would kindly
bring a message for us to the police. We have heard that we
cannot go through the village. There are men with guns waiting for us. If you don't do this it means that we must go back
over the mountain, tramp many miles and take a boat across
the bay; always provided that we can get a boat. And we have
no food. But if you would just give a note to the police
sergeant, he would come out here for us. It is easy for you;
no one will molest you. You can get through safely.'

The hawker reflected before replying. Then with obvious
hesitation he spoke:

'I would gladly help you, ma'am. But you see how it is.
It is true that the people here like me and trust me. But what
would happen to me if they saw me stop at the barracks, if
they found out that I was going there with messages? I
must think of my own. And they would surely find out. I
don't know how, but they find out everything. They have
eyes at the back of their heads, ears in every place. I could
take your note and destroy it, but it is better that I tell you
the truth. I cannot bring a message. What would Rachel do,
what would my son and my two daughters do, if I were
killed? You are asking too much of me. All I can do is tell
no one I've seen you.'

'You have two daughters. So have I, but I have no son.'
The woman's voice was honey-sweet. It stirred the hawker in
a strange way.

'You are young,' he said, in a comforting tone, 'Who
knows, perhaps you will have many sons.'

'I never greatly wanted a son. At first perhaps, when I
was just married. Now I am pleased to be the mother of
daughters. What do men do in this world but cause trouble
and heartbreak? My daughters are lovely little creatures, like
flowers. I love watching them play in the garden. One has
yellow hair and one brown. They roll over and over on the
grass like two little kittens. I could not love a boy as I love

my two sweet little daughters. They belong to me, you see.
A boy belongs to his father.'

'Why do you not stay with your children then? It is
dangerous and rough the life you lead, tramping the roads
like a pedlar. Besides they need you.'

'No, my mother is with them always. I don't travel the
roads because I like doing it. It is terrible but it was a
thousand times worse before. At night, when my husband
was away, I could not sleep. My existence was a nightmare.
I would wander round the house, go into the children's room
and look at them lying asleep in their beds. And I would ask
myself what would we do, they and I, if he should be killed.
I could see him lying dead in a ditch, my babies orphans,
unprotected. And for them I want every good thing in life.
I want them to be strong and happy, and secure. It does not
matter for myself. I do not care very much even for James.
But my two children, they must not be left without help,
without protection. So I came with him. He is safer if I am
there. I can stand between him and harm and I can shoot
like a man. I can ride, row a boat, help in a thousand ways.
And then people respect me. These peasants admire courage.
They even fear me to some extent, a woman who has no fear
of death. Some even think I am a witch.'

'Why does your husband do this work then? Surely he
could find other things to do. He could be a lawyer or a
doctor. There are many occupations he could find and then
you could stay at home with your children. You should be
happy by your hearth, teaching them to sew and cook.'

'He likes this life of danger. At home he is restless. He
wanders about with his gun and dogs, gloomy and sullen.
He never asks himself what others feel. When I see a family
evicted, I sit down and weep, my heart full of sorrow, thinking of some poor mother with no home for her children. He
does not realize they are human beings. He never troubles
to think of my sufferings. He never thinks of his children.
Men, most men are like that. They must live their lives for
themselves. He permits me to accompany him because I am
useful. Not because I cannot rest at home when he is not
there.'

'Would it not be worse if your children were left without

their mother too?'

'No one will touch me. I know I am safe. And even if by some evil chance I should be killed, they will then be cared for. My mother is there to attend to them, and the world will pity them more, doubly orphaned. But I have no fear of that. No one will lift a hand against me, even if I were to shoot. But tell me about your two daughters. What age are they? Are they dark or fair? Are they pretty?'

The woman's voice was low and singing, honey-sweet. The hawker was moved by it in some way he did not understand.

'My two daughters,' he said unevenly and as if he spoke unwillingly, 'They are good girls. Miriam is twelve and already can cook and sew wonderfully. Anna is ten. She is very gay and lively, always making fun of her father. When I come home, they run to meet me and look in my pockets to see what I have brought them. They are so grown-up and dignified when they go out for a walk with their mother, but at home they are just little children. They sit on my knee and pull my beard and ask for stories. They take good care of their little brother. They bring him to school every day. Some day I must find them good husbands. Then I will be able to sit quietly at home and see all the young people about me. It is a good thing to grow old surrounded by many children.'

'Some day, if we get back to Derry safely, I should like to come and see them. Perhaps they might like to come to my home and play in the garden with Tess and Evelin. I'd like that very much. Do you know, Evelin is very intelligent, more intelligent than Tess, but Tess is sweeter. Evelin, the rascal, makes her sister do everything she wants. She just leads her round on a string. Sometimes poor Tess gets so worried at it that she comes in and sits down beside me and won't play any more. But she soon forgets, jumps up and runs after her sister, shouting, "Come on, Evie, I'll let you be the mother".'

'Ah, what a pity you cannot be with them always.'

'But I am tiring you,' said Eleanor Spain. 'You have a long walk tomorrow. Perhaps your wife is anxious for you now. And she will be worried if you come home ill and tired. Go to sleep. I must sleep too. For the road over the mountain is a long one and we will be two nights in the open, even if we should find a boat and get home. Sleep.'

'Sleep well!' said the hawker gently, leaning over to pile more hay over the woman.

But he did not sleep. He lay wide awake in the darkness, staring at the door of the barn. Dimly he could see James Spain's figure, standing there, motionless, keeping watch. The woman's voice still lingered in his ears, disturbing him. He could see her, dressed in a soft, white summer dress, throwing a coloured ball to her children, who rolled over and over in the grass like two kittens. He turned and twisted in the hay, trying to make himself more comfortable, as if he might thereby induce sleep.

The wind continued howling, but more fitfully. It had spent its anger. After a little while the hawker bent forward and touched the woman.

'Are you asleep?' he asked.

'No.'

'Soon I'll fall asleep. If, when I am asleep you put a letter into my boot, I shall know nothing about it. I will take off my boot as I pass the police barracks, for it will be hurting me. I'll shake it out, do you understand?'

'Yes, I understand. I thank you with all my heart. My children will thank you. I will bring them to see you when we are all of us home.'

'Don't thank me, please. I am doing nothing, nothing at all. Sleep, sleep in peace.'

The hawker turned round and soon his loud breathing sounded through the barn.

When he awoke in the morning, very early, the storm had ceased. A strong wind was still blowing gustily. He shouldered his pack, and going to the barn door, looked out. The whole world looked fresh and young. There was joy in his heart.

James Spain was sitting near the door, cleaning his revolver. He looked up, but did not say one word, merely nodded his head. Eleanor Spain hurried forward and took the hawker's hand. She smiled at him and said in a low, gentle voice, 'It is a man like you I should have chosen, a man of peace. God go with you!'

But the hawker did not hear what she said, did not notice the smile. Only the soft singing sound of her voice lingered in his ears as he tramped down the hill.

There's one born every minute

The crowd had vanished from Platform 1. After the bustle and rush of the arrival there was a sudden quiet, interrupted only by the whistles of shunting engines and the lazy calls of the porters who were shifting the last few packages. Dan Spain, who had been looking at the scene, shrugged his shoulders and walked slowly towards the Underground.

He felt a tap on his shoulder. He turned round abruptly, his eyes opened wide in apprehension. He saw, however, not the policeman he had expected, but a tall well-dressed Johnnie-about-town. Danny looked him over from the crown of his grey trilby to the toes of his highly polished shoes, all in such shining contrast to his own shabby outfit. But in the flicker of the blue eyes which looked into his own, he recognized a brother.

'I beg your pardon,' said the Johnnie. He had a soft ingratiating accent with just a hint, the merest hint of a brogue. 'Do you know if the Irish Mail has come in yet?'

Danny nodded in the direction of the steaming engine and remarked curtly: 'A quarter of an hour ago. There she is. Came in on the dot.'

The Johnnie frowned: 'Really, this is most distressing. I was to have met a friend of mine and gone down to Oxford with him. Now he hasn't turned up. How annoying! And there is no train until tomorrow morning. What on earth am I to do? I left home this morning in such a hurry that I forgot my pocket book.'

He slapped his breast pocket with an embarrassed laugh.

Danny looked at the handsome stranger coldly. Then

tapping him gently on the shoulder he replied grimly, 'Put a sock in it, friend.'

The young man blushed becomingly and stammered, 'I know it sounds funny, but still . . .'

'Funny,' exclaimed Danny. 'Phoney, if you like. Listen, stranger. Your Papa was rolling that one when you were still wet behind the ears. Put a sock in it, I tell you. You can't play me for a sucker.'

'But really!' expostulated the Johnnie.

'See here,' said Danny with a confidential wink, 'I came here to meet my mother and she didn't show up either. Come along and have a drink.'

'I don't mind if I do,' said the Johnnie, 'I've had an exhausting day.'

'That's better,' said Danny. 'Dog shall not eat dog, as they say where I come from.'

'And where might that be?' asked the stranger falling into step beside Danny.

'Not so far from your own town-land, I'm thinking. You see before you stranger, Danny Spain, born in the Coombe, in the city of Dublin, citizen of the world. I've hoboed it in Canada, panhandled up and down every State in the Union, beat it down to Rio, played the race courses in the Argentine, and I know every dosshouse in Sydney. And you thought you could play *me* for a sucker! You're a Dublin man yourself?'

'Sure,' replied the Johnnie, his elegant accent dropping from him like a cloak, 'Born in Fitzwilliam Square, went to Clongowes and Trinity. Name's Laurence Tibbald.'

'Well!' remarked Danny, 'It's as far a cry from Fitzwilliam Square to the Coombe as it is from Euston to Rio, but here we are. What are you having?'

'Irish and water.'

Danny gave the order to the barmaid. They took their drinks and moved over to the side table.

Danny pushed back his tattered hat, drew his hand down over his face and lifting his glass, exclaimed: 'Health and prosperity, Larry, and may the devil take the hindmost!'

'Good health!' said Larry.

They lit cigarettes and sat for a few minutes looking at

one another, each sizing the other up much as dogs do when they meet.

'You seem to have travelled a bit,' Larry remarked at last. 'You must have had a bit of fun here and there.'

Danny grinned.

'You're telling me, stranger. I'm an old hand. Plump me down in any quarter of this old globe and inside an hour I'll have my bearings all mapped out. I'll know just what line to take. I tell you, I'm an artist at the game, no flies on Dan Spain. The only soft thing about me is my corn. Oh, there have been ones who thought to best me, but where are they now? Improving their education in the hoosegow. And where am I? Right at the top of the line.'

Larry smiled.

'Well, you know, you affect a very good disguise.'

'Sure,' said Danny, stroking his chin with the finger and thumb of his left hand. 'Disguise is the word. Never let yourself be noticed. Now there's them that puts on a disguise that wouldn't take in a blind pup. They lay it on extra, so to speak. False nose over their own, false hair over their own. Or else they get themselves up regardless like yourself, too good to be true, if you catch my point.'

'I think I do,' said Larry.

'Good, now take yourself. Now what you should do to play your line is to look shabby and respectable, clean and honest. Nothing looks so genuine and decent as a clean shirt rather the worse of wear and shoes a bit dusty. You go away and sell that hat to someone who plays with rabbits and get yourself a good tweed suit, second hand, and you'll look the ticket.'

'You really think so?'

'Sure thing,' said Danny. 'Protective colouring they call it. Now one time down in Santos — were you ever in Santos, mister?'

'Not yet,' said Larry.

'Well, I'd jumped my ship at Santos. I was waiting for another to take me down to Buenos Ayres. One evening I got into a bit of a rumpus, right slap in the middle of it. We were in the Monkey Cafe, you've heard of the place, or maybe you haven't, it doesn't matter anyway. It was all a little question

of there being an extra ace in the pack. And those dagoes
are quick with their knives. Quick? I'll tell the world they're
quick. They'd slice your ear off hot before you'd have time
to crack an egg. The crowd was mixed. Squareheads off the
ships, Polak steevedores, Scotch engineers, and Dagoes.
Before we knew the whole place was surrounded by the
Vigilantes. You know their dodge? They just run you in till
the Captain comes to get you out, at your own expense, of
course. They dispense with the trial. No beaks down there.
And say, did you ever see the inside of a Brazilian gaol?
Well, sonny, there are good gaols and bad gaols, but the
Brazilian ones are in a class all to themselves. Ever been in
the clink?'

'No,' said Larry almost apologetically, 'not yet.'

'Well, you will if you go on the way you're doing. They'll
get wise to your little game in next to no time. Well, as I was
saying, there was the cafe all surrounded by the Vigilantes,
dirty looking customers, armed to the teeth. I was dressed
like any beachcomber and no one would guess by the look of
me that I had about twenty pounds in Brazilian reis on me.
I wriggled out of the swarm. There was a frightful row
going on, men and women screaming in every language under
the sun, and that blasted monkey, perched up on his ring
over our heads, screaming louder than any dago of them all.
I made for the door. Two Vigilantes there. I looked at them
as if I were blind drunk or full of snow, waving my hand
careless-like over my head. They let me pass, thinking I was
just a bum down and out, cadging drinks. I staggered very
slowly across the street and into a house on the other side.'

Danny leant back in his chair, thumbs in the armholes of
his waistcoat and beamed at Larry.

'Close thing!' remarked Larry.

'I'll say it was. Now if you'd been there, you'd have had
about as much chance as a hot dog in Iceland. With that
fancy suit on your back they'd be sure to think you had
plenty of dough on you. And you'd be most likely still killing
bugs in a Brazilian hoosegow.'

'Very likely,' said Larry, 'I'm too raw. I can see that. What
line are you working now? Surely with all your experience
you ought to have a better lay than the railway stations.'

'I'm playing safe. The flat racing hasn't begun yet. You see the higher you play, the bigger your profits, but the expenses are bigger. If you're peddling phoney shares down in the city, well you may get away with a lot, but just the same you may get away with seven years hard too, but the most they can do now is run me in on a minor charge like having no visible means of support.'

'What card are you playing, though?'

'The hard luck story. And I make it a good one. Never a word of a lie. I look out for some decent woman getting out of the train looking a bit strange and nervous. First time in the great city. If no one is meeting her I go right up to her and ask her if she's seen an old woman coming over all alone. Then I reel off a description of my old mother. I'm a bit worried. Then I turn round and help the woman. I bring her to a decent place, a genuine decent place. I carry up her bag and talk to her about home. I say maybe it's just as well the old woman didn't come as I'm out of a job. Maybe in a day or two things will be better. I might manage to get my dress suit out of pawn and get a job as a waiter. There's a job waiting for me. So as like as not the good woman stumps up the money for me. At the worst she gives me half a crown for my trouble and a lot of good advice. I'm good at listening to advice. There's often a lot in it.'

'It doesn't seem very ambitious,' said Larry, 'not for a man of your capabilities.'

'I know,' sighed Danny, 'but it's safe. I have my own reasons for keeping out of the hands of the police. You see once you come under their notice they sit heavy on your track until they get something on you, something that'll send you down for a long spell. You're a marked man. So I say to you, as a friend, get rid of that fancy suit or keep it for attending weddings. You can often pick up something good at a wedding.'

'It's kind of you to put me wise like this,' said Larry, 'I'm handicapped by not knowing.'

'Oh, that's nothing. I've a kind heart. But tell me now how you came into this racket. You see, I was kind of born to it. Began getting the better of other chislers in the street and just extended my territory. But you now, surely with your education and your people you could have done something better. Anyone can see you're a mug at the game.'

'Well,' said Larry, twisting his cigarette and looking at it in a shy and embarrassed way, 'I left college before I had finished because, well, the old man died. I went into my uncle's firm, and well, you see, I didn't get on with him very well. A tough old guy. He knew my mother was depending on me, so he drove me all the harder. You know the sort.'

'I know,' said Danny, 'full of good advice for the poor. Always telling you how to live on tuppence a week and the smell of an oil-rag.'

'Just so. Then I began playing the races, you know how it is and had hard luck. Got shot out on my ear. I had some decent clothes still and a few pounds so I came across, hoping to get something decent. I don't mind much for myself. I'd do any kind of work, but, you know how it is. I must send my mother some money and I must pretend I am in a decent job, have a respectable address and so on. As a matter of fact there's an old school friend of mine in Birmingham and he's doing well. He wrote to me asking me to come down and he'd see me fixed. I was to have met him here, but he didn't show up. If I had the fare to get down there, I'd be set fair and square and well, you know, it would about kill my mother if she found out what's happened to me. I live in hourly dread, indeed I do.'

Danny looked at Larry sympathetically.

'That's hard luck,' he said. 'I tell you what, I'll stake you your fare. You can post it back to me when you're settled.'

He took a dirty sheet of paper out of his pocket, scribbled his name and address on it and handed it over with a pound note. Larry took it with a certain show of reluctance.

'Thanks, Danny,' he said almost roughly, 'You're a decent man. You'll have it back in a couple of days.'

He got up and gave Danny his hand.

'Good luck,' said Danny grimly.

Larry hurried away. Danny looked after him, an expression of sad disgust on his face.

After a while he moved towards the bar and asked for another drink. As he took it he looked at the barmaid and remarked: 'Dog shall not eat dog'.

'Pardon?' asked the girl mystified.

'I was saying,' said Danny, 'Old Barnum was right, there's one born every minute.'

'Quite,' said the young woman.

Village without Men . . . .

Weary and distraught the women listened to the storm as it raged around the houses. The wind screamed and howled. It drove suddenly against the doors with heavy lurchings. It tore at the straw ropes which anchored the thatched roofs to the ground. It rattled and shook the small windows. It sent the rain in narrow streams under the door, through the piled-up sacks, to form large puddles on the hard stamped earthen floors.

At times when the wind dropped for a moment to a low whistling whisper and nothing could be heard but the hammering of the sea against the face of Cahir Roe, the sudden release would be intolerable. Then one or another would raise her head and break into a prayer, stumbling words of supplication without continuity or meaning. Just for a moment a voice would be heard. Then the screaming wind would rise again in fury, roaring in the chimney and straining the roof-ropes, the voice would sink to a murmur and then to nothing as the women crouched again over the smouldering sods, never believing for a moment in the miracle they prayed for.

Dawn broke and the wind dropped for a while. The women wrapped their shawls tightly round them, knotted the ends behind them and tightened their headcloths. They slipped out through cautiously opened doors. The wind whipped their wide skirts so tightly to their bodies it was hard to move. They muttered to themselves as they clambered over the rocks or waded through the pools down to the foaming sea.

To the right Cahir Roe sloped upward, smothered in storm clouds, protecting the village from the outer sea. The ears of the women rang with the thunder of the ocean against its giant face. Salt foam flecked their faces, their clothes as they struggled along in knots of three or four, their heads turned from the wind as they searched the shore and looked out over the rolling water. But in all that grey-green expanse of churning sea, nothing. Not even an oar. All day long they wandered.

It was not until the turn of the tide on the second day that the bodies began to roll in, one now, another again, over and over in the water like dark, heavy logs. Now a face showed, now an outstretched hand rose clear of the water. John Boyle's face had been smashed on the rocks, yet his wife knew him as an incoming wave lifted his tall lean body to hurl it to shore.

For two days the women wandered until the ocean, now grown oily but still sullen with anger, gave up no more. Niel Boylan, Charley Friel and Dan Gallagher were never found.

The women rowed across the bay to the little town of Clonmullen for the priest. After the heavy rain the road across the bog was dangerous, and the village was cut off by land. The young curate, Father Twomey, came across. When he looked at the grey haggard faces of these women, all words of comfort deserted the young priest. His throat went dry and his eyes stung as if the salt sea had caught them. What comfort could words bring to women in their plight? He could with greater ease pray for the souls of the drowned than encourage the living to bear their sorrow in patience.

The women had opened the shallow graves in the sandy graveyard. They lowered the bodies and shovelled back the sand. Then for headstones, to mark the place where each man was laid before the restless sand should blot out every sign, they drove an oar which he had handled into each man's grave and dropped a stone there for every prayer they said. The wind blew the sand into the priest's vestments, into his shoes, into his well-oiled hair and into his book. It whirled the sand around the little heaps of stones.

As the women rowed him home across the bay, the priest looked back at the village. The oars in the graves stood out against the stormy winter sky like the masts of ships in harbour.

The midwife was the first to leave the village.

As they brought each dead man up from the sea, she stripped him and washed his body. For most of them she had done this first service. From early youth, first with her mother, then alone, she had plied her trade on this desolate spit of land. These same bodies which once warm, soft, tender and full of life, had struggled between her strong hands, now lay cold and rigid beneath them. She washed the cold sea-water from these limbs from which she had once washed the birth-slime. Silently she accomplished her task and retired to her cottage. Of what use was a midwife in a village without men?

She wrote to her married daughter in Letterkenny who replied that there was work in plenty for her there. Then two weeks later when the hard frosts held the bog road, she loaded her goods on a cart and set out for Clonmullen from where she could get the train to Letterkenny. She took with her young Laurence Boyle, John Boyle's fourteen-year-old son, to bring back the donkey and cart.

The women watched her go. A few called God-speed but the others, thin-lipped, uttered no word. Silently they went back to their houses and their daily tasks. From now on their bodies would be barren as fields in winter.

All winter the village lay dumb and still. The stores of potatoes and salt fish were eaten sparingly. The fish might run in the bay now, followed by the screaming seagulls, but there were no men to put out the boats or draw in the gleaming nets. The children gathered mussels to feed the hens.

Then in the early spring days, the women rose from their hearths, and tightly knotted their headcloths and shawls. They took down the wicker creels from the lofts, the men's knives from the mantleshelves and went down to the rocks below Cahir Roe to cut the seawrack for the fields. The children spread it on the earth. Then with fork and spade the women turned the light sandy soil, planted their potatoes, oats and barley. The work was heavy and backbreaking but it had to be done. If they did not work now with all their strength, their children would be crying for food in the coming winter.

Driven, bone-tired, sick at heart, they rose early and worked all day, stopping at midday as their husbands had stopped, to rest in the shelter of a stone wall, to drink some milk or cold tea and to eat some oatbread the children brought to them in the fields. At night they dragged their bodies to bed. There was no joy, no relief to be got there now. Nothing but sleep, easing of weary muscles.

Their work in the house was neglected. The hearths went untended, their clothes unwashed. They no longer white-washed the walls of the cottages or tended the geraniums they grew in pots. They did not notice when the flowers died.

The next to leave the village was Sally Boyle. She was to have married young Dan Gallagher after the next Lent. There at the end of the straggling village was the half-built ruin of the house he had been getting ready with the help of the other men in the village. All winter she moped over the fire, only rousing herself when her mother's voice rose sharp and angry. Now in the spring she began to wander about restlessly. She would leave her work and climb the great headland of Cahir Roe, there to look out to where Tory rose like a fortress from the sea — out there across the sea in which Dan Gallagher had been drowned, the sea which had refused to surrender what should have been hers. At night in bed she could not control the wildness of her body. She pitched from side to side, moaning and muttering. Her whole mind was darkened by the memory of soft kisses on warm autumn nights, of strong hands fondling her. She felt bereft, denied.

She slipped away one day and joined the lads and lasses in Clonmullen who were off to the hiring fair at Strabane. Later her mother got a letter and a postal order for five shillings. Sally was now hired girl on a farm down in the Lagan.

Then in ones and twos the young girls began to leave. With the coming of spring their eyes brightened, their steps grew lighter. They would stop and look over their shoulders hurriedly as if someone were behind. They would rush violently to work and then leave their tasks unfinished to stand and look out over the landscape, or out to sea from under a sheltering hand. They became irritable, quarrelsome and penitent by turns. Somewhere out there across the bog, across the sea, lay a world where men waited; men who could marry them, love them perhaps, give them homes and children.

The women objected to their going and pleaded with them. Every hand was needed now. The turf must be cut in the bog, turned and stacked for the coming winter. Surely they could go when the crops were gathered in. But tears and pleading were in vain. Nature fought against kindness in their young bodies. Here no men were left to promise these girls life, even the hazardous life of this country. They gathered their few garments together and departed, promising to send back what money they could. But their mothers knew that it was not to get money they left. It was the blood in their veins which drove them forth. And though the women lamented, they understood.

No use now to give a dance for the departing girls. There were no men with whom they could dance. No use to gather the neighbours into the house to sing. The voices of women are thin and shrill without men's voices to balance them.

Larry Boyle found himself the only lad in the village. The other boys were many years younger and those who were older had been lost with their fathers in the storm. The winter gloom, the silence of the women and his loneliness drove him to day-dreaming, to the creation of a fantasy world. He saw himself, in coming years, stronger and taller than any man, towering over humanity as Cahir Roe towered over the sea, impregnable, aloof. Boats, fields, cattle, houses, everything in the village would belong to him. For as yet the outside world meant nothing to him and women had no power over his dreams. They existed but to serve him.

At first the women paid no more attention to him than they did to the other children. He ate what food was set before him. Some potatoes, a piece of dried salt fish, a bowl of buttermilk. He performed such tasks as were set him, helping with the few cows, carrying the seawrack, heeling the turf. Indeed he was despised rather than otherwise, for the girls of his age were more nimble and less absent-minded than he. But slowly, as if in answer to his dreams, his position changed. In every house he entered he was welcomed and given the seat by the fire. He was never allowed to depart without food and drink. The older women baked and cooked for him, kept the best for him, gave him small presents from their hoard; a husband's knife; a son's trousers. They began to compliment him at every turn on his strength and growth. No one asked him to work.

Now he allowed his hair to grow like a man's. The stubby quiff vanished and a crop of thick, fair curls crowned his forehead, giving him the obstinate look of a fierce young ram. He became particular about the cleanliness of his shirt, refused to wear old patched trousers and coats. Gradually he dominated the whole village. Even the dogs owned him sole master, and snarled savagely at one another when he called them to heel. The younger boys were his slaves, to fetch and carry for him. He scarcely noticed the girls of his own age, never called them by name, never spoke directly to them. Unlike them, he had no wish to leave the village.

A day came when Larry Boyle went from house to house and collected the fishing lines, hooks and spinners which had belonged to the drowned men. They were granted him as if by right. He took them to the rock behind the village where formerly the fish had been dried and where the men had then met in the summer evenings to talk, away from their women-folk. It was a day of shifting sun and shadow and the wind from the west broken by the headland.

He sang as he carefully tested, cut and spliced each line. He rubbed the hooks and spinners clean of rust with wet sand from the stream. He made a long line, tested each length and wound it in a coil between hand and elbow. He fastened the hooks and the lead weight. Then, satisfied, he went down to the shore to dig bait.

He swung his can of bait over his shoulder, picked up his line and made for Cahir Roe. He was going to fish for rock-fish.

A deep shelf ran round part of the headland and from this the men had fished in the drowsy heat of summer days when they could spare time from the fields. He clambered along the shelf and stood on the edge. The sea heaved and foamed beneath him. Far out, Tory rose, a castle against the white line of the horizon.

He fixed his bait carefully and placed the loose end of the line beneath his heel. Then, clear of the beetling rock behind, he swung the coil of line above his head and threw it far out. His body, balanced over the edge, seemed to follow it as his eye watched the untwisting of the cord, the drop of the lead towards the sea. He bent down and gathered up the end.

He could feel the movement as the length of line ran through the sea and the weight sank slowly through the heavy water. His hand knew what was happening down there beneath the surface of the water. He felt the lead strike the bottom. His fingers, born to a new delicacy, held the line firmly so that the bait should float free. He could feel the gentle nibbling of the fish at the bait, nibbling cautiously, daintily, as sheep nibble grass. Twice he drew in his line to rebait the hook. Then one struck.

Excited, breathing heavily, his eyes distended, he drew in the line slowly, letting it fall in careful coils at his feet. Then the fish left the water and the full weight hung on the line. It plunged about madly in the air, twisting and flapping. The cord rubbed against the edge of the shelf as it passed from hand to hand, dislodging small stones and dirt from the crumbling surface. He had to lean out to jerk the fish over the edge, at that moment unaware of everything but the twisting, flapping fish. He threw it well behind him so that it could not leap back into the water. It lay there, twisting and turning, its brilliant orange and green colouring coming and going, its belly heaving, its panting gills shining red. Then it lay still and from its open mouth the brick-red blood flowed over the stones. Another leap, another twitch. It was dead.

Larry passed the back of his hand across his forehead to wipe away the sweat. Before he stooped to disengage the hook from the jaws of the fish, he looked around him, at Tory on the far horizon, at the towering cliff above, the heaving sea beneath. For a moment his head reeled as he felt the turning of the world.

The women liked the new schoolmistress. They liked her modesty and reserve. Though young she knew how to keep the children in order, teach them their lessons and their manners. They looked after her with approval when they saw her walk precisely from the school to the cottage where she lived, her hands stiffly by her sides, her eyes lowered. They admired her round, rosy face, her light hair, her neat figure. She appeared so young and lovely to these women whose bodies were lean and tired from hard work and poor food.

She never stopped at the half-door for a chat, nor delayed for a moment to pass the time of day with a neighbour on the road. She never played with the younger children. She walked around encased in herself.

Every Saturday while the road held, she would mount her clean, well-oiled bicycle and cycle to Clonmullen. On the way she did not speak to anyone nor answer a greeting. With gaze fixed on the road before her, she pedalled furiously. In Clonmullen she would make one or two purchases, post her letters and cycle back home. All attempts at conversation were firmly repulsed. She did not even stop to have tea at the hotel.

She lived alone in a small cottage built on the rise of ground just beyond the village. For an hour at a time she would kneel in the shelter of the fuchsia hedge and gaze hungrily at the houses she did not wish to enter, at the women to whom she did not care to speak. She knew all their comings and goings, all the details of their daily life. She watched them at their work, in their conversation. She watched the children at play. She watched Larry Boyle as he wandered along the shore towards Cahir Roe to fish, or passed her cottage on his way to set rabbit snares in the burrows.

The July heat beat down on the earth and the blue-grey sea moved sleepily under a mist. He was returning home when he saw her, standing in the shelter of the bushes that grew over the gateway. She was looking at him with fierce intentness. He stood still and gazed back, his eyes wide and startled. The fear of unknown lands, of uncharted seas took hold of him. His mouth dropped open, his skin twitched. His throat hurt and there was a hammering in his ears like the heavy pounding of the surf on Cahir Roe. He could not move hand nor foot. With a sudden movement her hand darted out and caught his wrist. She drew him towards her, in the shelter of the thick fuchsia hedge. Frightened by her intent stare, her pale face, her quick uneven breathing, when she put out her other hand to fondle him, he pulled away and burst through the bushes. Quietly, with lowered eyes, she listened as his boots clattered over the rocky road. She sighed and turned back into her house.

But he came back. Furtively. He would steal into her kitchen when she was at school and leave some offering; a freshly caught fish, a rabbit, some rock pigeon's eggs. He had so little to give. She did not seem to notice. She did not stop him to thank him when they met. She passed without even a greeting, once again encased in her rigid calm. Then one evening, as darkness fell, he lifted the latch of her door. She was seated on her hearthrug, gazing at the glowing turf fire. He approached in silent desperation and with the same wild desperation she answered.

Such happenings do not long remain hidden in a small world. Without a word spoken, the women came to know. Primitive anger seized hold on them. They said nothing to Larry. Their belief in man's place in life and the fact that they had denied him nothing shut their mouths. All their rage turned against the young teacher whom they had thought so modest and gentle. They became as fierce as hawks at the theft of their darling.

They ceased work. They came together in groups, muttering. They buzzed like angry bees. Their lips spoke words to which their ears were long unaccustomed as they worked themselves into an ancient battle fury. They smoothed their hair back from their foreheads with damp and trembling hands. They drew their small shawls tightly round their shoulders.

From behind the fuchsia hedge the girl saw them coming like a flock of angry crows. Their wide dark skirts, caught by the light summer breeze, bellowed out behind them. Their long, thin arms waved over their heads like sticks in the air. Their voices raised in some primitive battle cry, they surged up the road towards her.

Terrified of this living tidal wave, she rushed out. The uneven road caught her feet. It seemed to her that she made no headway as she ran, that the surging mass of women came ever nearer. Stones rattled at her heels. She ran on in blind panic, unaware of where she was going. Her chest began to ache, her throat to burn. A stone caught her shoulder but she scarcely felt the blow. Then another hit her on the back and she stumbled. Still she ran on, not daring to look back. A stone struck her head. She reeled and fell. Over the edge of the narrow bog road, down the bank towards the deep watery ditch. Briars caught her clothes. Her hands grasped wildly at the tufts of rough grass. There she lay, half in, half out of the water, too frightened to move or struggle.

When they saw her fall, the women stopped and stood there in the road, muttering. Then they turned back. They burst into her neat little cottage. They threw the furniture about, broke the delft, hurled the pots out of doors, tore the pretty clothes to ribbons. Then they left, still muttering threats, like the sea after storm.

Later, shivering, aching, sick, the girl dragged herself back onto the road. There was no one there now. The flock of crows had gone. She stood alone on the empty road. There was no sound but the lonely call of a moor bird overhead.

The next day Larry, too, left the village.

The war when it came meant little to these women. The explosions of mines on the rocks could not harm them now that there were no men to risk their lives on the water. The aeroplanes which from time to time circled over the coast seemed to them no more than strange birds, at first matter for wonder and then taken for granted. Sometimes the sea washed up an empty ship's boat, some timbers or empty wooden cases. One morning scores of oranges came dancing in on the waves. The children screamed with delight and, not knowing what they were, played ball with them. But since the oranges did not bounce they soon tired of them and left them along the shore to rot. The women only realized that the war could touch them when the supplies of Indian meal ran out.

All that winter storms lashed the coast. Snow whirled around the houses, blotting out the sight of the fierce sea which growled savagely against the headland of Cahir Roe day and night. Not once during the bitter months did the snow melt on the mountains beyond Clonmullen. The wind tore at the ropes which tethered the thatched roofs, rotting and grass-grown from neglect. The north-east wind drove under the doors, roared in the chimneys; it hardened the earth until it was like a stone.

Yet now it seemed that the silence was broken, that terrible silence they had kept in mourning for their dead. Now in the evenings they gathered round one another's firesides. They told stories, old Rabelaisian tales heard when they were children from the old men of the village. Such tales as lie deep in the minds of people and are its true history. Tales of old wars, of great slaughter of men, of the survival of the women and children, of tricks to preserve the race. They told of the Danes and their love of the dark-haired Irishwomen. They laughed quietly and spoke in whispers of the great power of the Norsemen's bodies, of the fertility of their loins.

Over and over again they told the story of the women of Monastir, who, when widowed and alone, lured with false lights a ship to their shore. What matter that their victims were dark-skinned Turks. Their need was great.

The eyes of the women grew large and full of light as they repeated these tales over the dying embers of their fires. A new ferocity appeared in their faces. Their bodies took on a new grace, grew lithe and supple. As the body of the wild goat becomes sleek and lovely in the autumn.

Spring came suddenly. After the weeks of fierce winds and wild seas, followed days of mild breezes and scampering sun-

shine. The women threw open their doors and stepped out
with light hearts. As they cut the seawrack for their fields,
they called to one another and sang snatches of old songs.
Sometimes one or another would stop in her work and look
out over the water at the sea-swallows dipping and skimming
over the surface of the water, at the black shags as they swam
and dived, at old Leatherwing standing in his corner in wait.
The older children laughed and shouted as they helped to
spread out the wrack on the fields. The younger ones
screamed as they ran along the shore and searched under the
rocks for crabs. They called and clapped their hands at the
sea-pies as they bobbed up and down on the waves.

On and on the children ran, their toes pink in the sea-
water. They chattered together like pies over each fresh
discovery. They travelled along the shore until they found
themselves out on the point of land beside Cahir Roe, facing
the open sea. There they stood and looked out to sea from
under sheltering hands.

For some minutes they stood and stared. Then in a body
they turned and ran towards the women, shouting all
together that out there, coming in closer every minute, was
a strange boat.

The women straightened their backs and listened. Even
before they understood what the children were shouting,
they let down their petticoats and started for the point.
There they stood in a group and stared, amazed that a boat
should put in on that inhospitable shore. Close in now, with
flapping sail, the boat came.

They could make out only one man and their eyes, used to
long searching over water, could see that he was lying across
the tiller. Was he alive or dead? Could he not see where he
was going? If he did not change his course now he would
fetch up on the reef below Cahir Roe. They rushed forward
to the water's edge and shouted. The man bent over the tiller
did not move. They continued to shout. They waded into the
sea until the water surged against their bodies and threatened
to overbalance them. Their dark skirts swirled round them in
the heavy sea as they shouted and waved their arms.

Then the man at the tiller slowly raised his head. He
looked around him, at the sea, at the screaming women, at

the great red granite face of Cahir Roe. With great effort he pulled his body upright and swung the tiller over. Then he fell forward again. Even before the keel had grounded on the gravel, the women had seized the boat and dragged it up onto the beach.

Six men lay huddled in the bottom of the boat. Great, strong men, now helpless. The women turned to the helmsman. He looked at them with dull, sunken eyes. He moved. He tried to speak. His grey face was stiff, his lips cracked.

'Scotland?' he asked and his voice was hoarse.

The women shook their heads. Then the man slowly lifted one hand, pointed to the men at his feet and then to himself.

'Danes. Torpedoed. Ten days.'

The women cried aloud as they lifted the heavy bodies of the men. Their voices sang out in wild exultation.

The Danes. The Danes were come again.

The Kindly Face

I have a kind face. I often wish I hadn't. Better be cursed with a squint, buck teeth, knock knees and no forehead than with a kind face. For mankind as a whole always believes that a kind face is the outward and visible sign of a kind heart. I haven't got a kind heart. Again I say it, I have not got a kind heart, just a weak mind. I am the sort of person who gets button-holed at parties, led into a corner by some foolish woman or other and told the story of her life. Has anyone ever heard more life stories than I have? I am a walking case-book. Do I like it? No and no and no. These outpourings are only of interest to the teller. That's where my weak mind comes in. I listen, with irritation in my heart, yet I listen. My kind face is absolutely incapable of showing the irritation I feel.

And it's not only the women, mind you. If a man asks me out to dinner, I know he wants to ask my advice. He never by any chance asks me out because he likes my company. He has something to tell me which he cannot tell anyone else. It has generally something to do with some other woman, often two other women, seldom more, because the Don Juans of this world do not confide. Desperation seals their lips. I listen, I reflect and then I tell him just what he wants to hear. I have long ago learned the futility of telling man or woman anything else. They don't listen or they think me a fool. I am weak-minded enough not to like being taken for a fool.

I remember on one occasion I ventured to give advice. I must have been more than usually irritated. Tony Elliot had

taken me out to dinner and over the coffee confided in me
his great problem, how to keep a woman in love with him
and yet curb her possessive proclivities. It differed not by a
hair's breadth from a hundred stories I had already heard. He
took my hand kindly in his and asked:

'What do you think I should do, Anne?'

'Cut and run,' I answered.

'Why?' His voice sounded hurt.

'Because if you don't, your solicitor will soon be asking
you if you ever exchanged letters.'

'Don't be cynical, dear. It doesn't suit you.'

And that's all the good I did. He dropped me flat and
hadn't even the grace to be sorry when the solicitor did
ask him that question.

I am the kind of person who is always stopped in the
street and asked the way. I am the kind of person of whom
children ask the time. I am the kind of person whose true
nature can only be judged by a blind man and most blind
people live in institutions. Old ladies ask me to steer them
through the traffic and then invite me home to tea. Mothers
consult me about their daughters, fathers about their sons,
wives about their husbands and husbands about — not about
their wives, much.

Once I thought, I'll get away from all this. I decided to
go and stay in an expensive hotel at some fashionable resort
where no one would notice me. I am not an outstanding
personality. In the throng of fashionable men and women I
might well be overlooked. So I was, for about a week. Then
first of all the chambermaid came to consult me about her
young man. I had noticed that she had been hanging about
my room at odd hours. She confided in me that she thought
he was being lured away from her by another girl, a girl who
wore spectacles. She herself could not see with spectacles on.
She had tried on a pair in a shop. But did I think that if she
bought a pair made of ordinary glass that it would bring him
back? I looked at the girl. She was a fine-looking creature,
good eyes, sound teeth, a splendid colour and wondered why
any man should pass her over. At the same time I felt
annoyed with her. When would women get over thinking that
their own personal life was of the slightest importance? I

replied kindly, however. I have got into the habit now. I said that with her personal attractions she had nothing to fear from her myopic rival. It was what she wanted to hear so she went away happy.

That evening as I sat in the lounge drinking my coffee, a woman of about fifty came over and introduced herself. To the strains of the sentimental music wailed out by a discreet orchestra, she told me the story of her life. I assure you she left very little out, for it was a long story. I was asked to sympathize with her because of the cruelty of her husband, his meanness and total incapacity to understand her, because of the heartlessness of her daughter who preferred to live alone and of her son who had allowed his wife to poison his mind against his mother. Her life was miserable and lonely, spent drifting from hotel to hotel.

'We women have a hard life,' she sighed.

I agreed. It was the easiest, in fact the only thing to do, but if only she could have seen my thoughts how shocked she would have been. I excused myself as soon as I decently could and went up to my room. Presently there was a knock on my door. I opened it, a young woman burst in and flung herself on my bed in floods of tears. I had noticed her several times in the dining-room and on the tennis courts. She seemed a gay, bright, carefree creature. For once I felt a certain sympathy. I was sure that she felt upset because she had lost her wrist-watch or her bag. I let her cry for a few minutes before I asked: 'What's the matter, my dear?'

She raised her head and pointed to her lip. It was slightly bruised and cut. She must have knocked herself against the door. But was that a reason for these tears?

'How did it happen?' I asked.

'Eric!' she sobbed.

'Eric? Who's Eric?'

'My husband. He . . . he hit me.'

'Why?'

'I do hope you'll forgive me telling you all this. But you looked so kind and I have no one here. I feel so . . . so deserted and miserable.'

My God, I thought, do they all learn this off, or does it just spring spontaneously from their hearts?

'You haven't told me yet why?'

'He said I was leading Tom on.'

'And were you?'

'Of course not. He just misunderstood. It was all so innocent. Then we had an awful row and he hit me. I never thought he would do it. I never thought he would strike a woman.'

'What did you do? Did you hit him back?'

She looked at me with tearful astonished eyes.

'No, of course not. I just walked out of the room. He ran after me but I pushed him away. He must feel very low at having struck a woman.'

I wanted to shake the girl. How could she be such a fool? For once I ventured a piece of advice.

'That was silly of you. Now he will have a sense of guilt. That's what makes people hate one another. If you go on like this he will loathe you in six months.'

'Why shouldn't he feel guilty if he has done something wrong?'

'Don't let's go into the rights and wrongs. No one could possibly sort them out. I'm talking sense. If you make him feel a low scoundrel, he'll become a low scoundrel. It's just human nature.'

I could see her face hardening.

'I can't, I really can't bring myself to accept such a cynical attitude. I'm sure you don't really believe it yourself.'

'Let me tell you, girl, before you finally make a mess of your marriage and your life, that people will always react to your opinion of them. Think them good, tell them they're good and they become good, at least to you. Tell them they're bad and cruel and they're bad and cruel. Tell them they're kind hearted and they are kind hearted. It's part of their vanity.'

She dried her eyes briskly and got up from the bed.

'I don't agree with you. The only thing to do is to make people feel wrong when they are wrong. Thanks for listening to me. I'm sorry I was so hysterical, but you see I have no one here in whom I can confide, and I thought you looked so kind.'

She left the room with the same dignity she had probably

assumed when her husband had been goaded into striking her. I sympathized with him.

<hr>

'Lives of Great Men . . . .'

<hr>

One day, my father, when on a visit to Dublin, came on a *Life of Napoleon* on the book barrows. He paid twopence for the exceedingly dusty volume and bore it away with him to read as he sat, lonely and rather lost, in the lounge of the Wicklow Hotel that evening. For Father was never a man for the bars, and plays bored him if they were not of an improving or educational turn.

The Life of Napoleon was well worth twopence from the point of letterpress alone. There were seven hundred closely printed pages, full of military, strategic and diplomatic detail, long letters and finally Napoleon's *Apologia pro Waterloo*. A less stout man than my father would have quailed before such a volume. But Father had never been known to blanch before an enemy. The book was tackled and conquered. It came home with him.

'How do you know where that book may have been before you bought it?' asked Mother. 'How do you know what disease mayn't be in it? It smells.'

Father refused to yield the volume to the destructive hands of my mother, whose whole life was a constant, though losing, battle against dirt, germs, and disease. Still, when he was out one day, she placed it in a closet with a sulphur candle and left it there for some hours. After that it smelled worse than ever, but Mother's mind was more at ease.

My father's constant complaint was that Mother had no education nor wish to acquire any. Like so many women of her generation and upbringing, she had shared with her sisters and younger brothers an ill-equipped and underpaid governess. Then she'd been 'finished' at a school in England. We took it on faith that she had learned French and Italian, though we never saw any signs of a proficiency in these languages; that she had learned to play the piano, which she never opened; that she had learned to paint and do fine needlework, though we never, thank God, saw any evidence of either. She was the best cook I have ever met and an excellent housekeeper. In her spare moments she read novels of the more romantic sort. Father strictly forbade any of us to look at them, saying they would rot our minds. They were, it seemed, Mother's form of tippling.

Those were the good old days before we had heard of Freud and psychological escape and sugar was one penny a pound. Well, if romantic novels were Mother's escape, Napoleon was Father's.

Father was one of those people who could never keep a good thing to himself. Whether it was a new way of planting carrots or bottling home-brewed wine, which he never drank himself but gave to unwilling visitors, he was all for sharing his knowledge with the world. Knowledge hidden was treasure hidden. Knowledge, like money, should be kept in circulation and so accumulate. Soon we all began to share in *The Life of Napoleon*.

I do not know what my sisters' reactions to Napoleon were. The effect of my father's intensive education seemed to be to give them psychological deafness. They grew up as cheerfully ignorant as Mother. But to this day I am violently anti-dictator and that is due entirely to my father's rising enthusiasm for Napoleon.

'You see,' he would say, making tracks with his fork on Mother's linen table-cloth, 'Napoleon foresaw the cutting of the Suez Canal and the opening up of a new route to India.' Deep incision with the fork. 'This was the reason for the campaign into Egypt.'

Mother's glance was fixed on the line drawn by the fork, with rigid fascination. Her face seemed to say as plainly as words, 'Do you realize that that table-cloth cost ten pounds and linen isn't getting any cheaper.'

'You're not listening, Elizabéth,' said my father sternly, his brown eyes flashing.

'Of course, I'm listening. The campaign in Egypt. Go on.'

Whenever Father accused Mother of not listening, she would deny it stoutly and repeat the last words he had said with the glibness of a schoolboy. This parrot-like repetition always made Father's words sound rather foolish. But women's cunning never stopped Father, no matter how it might hamper and aggravate him. Was he not, after all, a sort of Napoleon himself?

He now addressed himself to his three daughters. With an ease born of long practice, they quietly and noiselessly continued to stuff their food into their mouths and listened with eyes wide open.

'He was probably the greatest genius the world has ever known, not merely as a general but as a ruler. But genius is always destroyed by mathematics. Wellington was mathematics . . .'

'He was an Irishman,' said my mother, as if that summed up the whole matter and put an end to further discussion.

Father paid no attention to this interruption.

'The *Code Napoleon* was a marvellous step in the direction of establishing social order, though, mind you, inferior to English Civil Law, since it presupposes the guilt of the accused and forces him to prove his innocence. In the English courts a man is innocent until he is proved guilty. But leaving that aside, it was a stupendous task for one man to accomplish.'

'He married one of the Pakenhams,' said my mother, 'Kitty Pakenham. My grandmother used to say that she was a sweet creature but very unhappy towards the end. The Pakenhams are from West Meath, like my grandmother's people. The two families were very friendly, and related in a way. It was my grandmother's uncle who married one of them.'

'Who married one of the Pakenhams?' roared my father.

'Why, my grandmother's Uncle George and the Duke of Wellington.'

'The same Pakenham?' Father's sarcasm was always of the heavy variety.

My mother cast her children a derisive glance as much as to say: 'I thought that would settle him.' But her children, ancients in guile, returned a blank stare.

'He discovered that sugar could be extracted from beet,' said Father to us.

'I wouldn't let a grain of it into the house,' said my mother. 'Nothing but the best cane sugar ever enters my pantry. I'm sure beet sugar is bad for the constitution and harmful for growing children. And God knows, good cane sugar should be within reach of all. Though I must say, it's never been the same since the Boer War. Nothing has. Even saucepans. Thank goodness, I've got some of my mother's. You never used to see any of those cheap enamel contraptions. Food doesn't taste the same out of them. And please, dear, don't destroy the table-cloth. The linen isn't the same either, now they bleach it with chemicals.'

'You never listen to a word I say,' roared Father.

'Yes, indeed I do. Extracted from beet. Go on.'

And believe me, he went on.

When it came to describing the battles, the pepper, salt, mustard and all available knives, forks and spoons were called into action.

'Here, on this slope, Napoleon stationed Junot.' He plonked down the pepper pot with a firm hand. 'And over here Marshall Nez.'

'Hetty dear,' Mother would say to my sister. 'Pass the mustard, please.'

My father's infuriated eyes would watch Marshall Nez travel to the other end of the table. In a moment he had him back.

'And the pepper, dear. I always think you need lots of pepper on cauliflower. The black kind. I don't approve of white pepper.'

'Even if you wish to remain ignorant yourself,' said Father bitterly, 'please allow me to instruct the children.'

'Indeed I am most interested. But I can't possibly eat meat without mustard, or cauliflower without pepper. Put Junot back, Hetty dear. Marshall Nez. Go on.'

'At this point Napoleon placed the heavy artillery. In this way he completely dominated . . .'

'Wasn't his second wife a Patterson?' asked my mother.

'Whose?' Father was fast losing control of his temper.

'Napoleon's. Isn't it Napoleon you're talking about? Didn't he marry a Patterson?'

'That was his brother.'

'That must have been a great relief to her family, that she didn't marry a divorced man. I wonder what Pattersons they were? A Dublin family, I think. It's a very mixed name. Still, it wasn't very nice for them to have a daughter marrying a foreigner.'

Month followed month and this still went on. My early years seemed blighted by Napoleon. There seemed to be no end to the books written on him and Father gathered them to himself, one by one. And as he read it, he retailed each in its turn, at meals. Mother's irrelevant interruptions continued. But they never did anything more than irritate Father. It was I who inadvertently put an end to the Napoleon.

My father's birthday was approaching, and I set out to buy him a present. I had one shilling, laboriously acquired. Father never gave us any money. He believed that money in the hands of women led to all manner of vice and reckless living, ending in the complete demoralization of the social order. I spent a whole afternoon wandering from one shop to another. I knew he would never wear a tie or socks which cost only one shilling. Father dressed expensively, no matter what his women-folk were forced by circumstances to wear. Everything I fancied cost at least two shillings and I knew that I had no hope whatever of acquiring the other shilling. I reached the stationer's and bookshop. They were well used to seeing me there. Since my hands, thanks to my mother's constant bullying were fairly clean, I was allowed to hang round the bookshelves and read.

I searched the sixpenny and shilling shelves for something on Napoleon. In vain. Then I took a book down and began to read it. I read on and on, fascinated. Closing-time came and I was still reading. I bought the book, thinking that Father would throw it aside and then I could take it back.

But I was wrong. Father, too, was fascinated. From Napoleon he passed on to whales.

And somehow I have never been able to finish *Moby Dick*.

The Voice that Breathed o'er Eden

Mrs. Brownrigg was a great believer in the married state. Indeed she had little reason to be otherwise, for Mr. Brownrigg, considerate soul that he was, had never, during his short span of married life, given her any cause for suspicion or regret. A humble man, his greatest flight of fancy never rose above a modest bet on a horse — and that only during office hours. Shortly after his marriage, which occurred late in life, his asthma overcame him. In halting accents he wheezed out: 'God bless you, my dear,' and died in her arms, leaving his widow amazed and disconsolate.

When, dressed in becoming widow's weeds, and seated beside the photograph of her late husband, she received the lawyer in her small Hampstead drawing-room, she was more than surprised at the respect with which he treated her. The surprise vanished, however, when she learnt that Mr. Brownrigg had left her very comfortably provided for. His estate to which she was the sole heir, amounted to some £12,724 - 6 - 4. She found it difficult to imagine what she could do with so much money. The lawyer talked securities and investments. She looked at him with that intelligent expression on her face which so many women can assume when they do not understand a word of what is being said to them. Sighing heavily and brushing away a tear with her black-bordered pocket-handkerchief, she said, 'I leave my affairs entirely in your hands, Mr. Cheeseman. If my dear husband thought you worthy of his trust and confidence, I cannot do better than follow his example.'

'I shall do everything, Mrs. Brownrigg,' murmured Mr.

Cheeseman in that low reverent voice common to lawyers and undertakers, 'everything within my power to deserve your high opinion of us.'

But now that Mr. Brownrigg had taken himself out of her life, Mrs. Brownrigg felt very lonely and melancholy. When her first grief had worn off, she noticed that many people who had been in the habit of asking her out with her husband, forgot her now. She felt herself in danger of becoming a lonely old woman with few interests and fewer friends. She took to brooding on the past, not gloomily, for her past had been a pleasant one. Yet her mind roved back to her youthful days in a Dorsetshire village, to memories of her mother, a very managing woman, the guiding light of the local Temperance Guild, the Church Restoration Fund and the Society for the Purification of the Young Person.

Suddenly she decided to sell her house in Hampstead and return home. She realized that with twelve thousand pounds she would be a much more important person in Little Muggleworth than in Hampstead where there were a great many widows with more natural advantages and even more money than she possessed.

She was lucky enough to be able to buy back her old home. She entered into her new life with spirit. The vicar and his wife called, of course, welcomed her back and made kindly yet discreet enquiries, such as a vicar and his wife are generally adepts at making. Mrs. Brownrigg, with the cunning of the truly simple woman, let it be understood that she was very rich indeed, and in less time than it took to get up all her new curtains, she had been elected on to all the possible committees. The vicar, without his wife, called to consult her on various questions and everyone was most careful not to ask her for money.

Whether it was the memory of her mother, or a natural interest in human frailty, there was none of her activities which interested her so greatly as her work for the Society for the Purification of the Young Person. Her discreet but confidential conversations with the vicar on the subject excited her tremendously, and though far be it from her to wish anyone harm, she always felt a certain thrill when a new case turned up. If the maiden in question were clever enough or lucky enough to lead her erring swain to the altar, Mrs. Brownrigg was always present at the ceremony, gave the bridal couple and the various relieved or sorrowing relatives a good wedding breakfast in her own dining-room and then presented the bride with five pounds. This five pounds had saved many a poor girl from a broken heart and tarnished honour.

Mrs. Brownrigg was a woman of vast energy and the passing years did not in any way curtail her interests, her curiosity and her capacity for interfering in other people's business. Nothing could happen in the village which did not somehow or other become known to her. She developed a passion for putting things right. She enjoyed telling the women how to deal with their drunken husbands and exhorted young maidens to guard well the most precious treasure of their womanhood. And though she was sometimes — in the privacy of the home — referred to as an old busy-body, the reputation she had acquired of being a woman of vast wealth and miserly propensities shut everyone's mouth in public. The vicar's wife invariably spoke of her as a 'sweet old soul'. The vicar acclaimed her as 'a great spirit', though, when together and sure that the maid was not listening, they lamented that she was overcareful with her money and showed a somewhat worldly spirit in regard to parting with it. They hoped, however, that her will was satisfactory — she could not live for ever, poor old dear. Concerning this, of course, they knew nothing, for Mrs. Brownrigg continued to trust and confide in Mr. Cheeseman and not in the local solicitor who might have dropped a kindly hint.

But Mrs. Brownrigg had one weakness. Everyone has and hers was a pardonable one. Her weakness was her gardener. As a gardener he showed no great brilliance. Her rose-garden never bloomed like that of the vicar's wife and her herbaceous border was nothing short of a scandal. Williams planted just what vegetables he wanted to grow and deeply resented it if they were borne away to the kitchen. He preferred them to go to seed. But Mrs. Brownrigg, though conscious of these shortcomings, felt that he amply compensated for them by the exemplary uprightness of his character. He never stopped at the village inn for a glass of beer and a game of darts. He never smoked. He knew no woman in marriage or otherwise. He lived with a maiden sister whom he bullied shamelessly and whom he never allowed to marry. This attitude, Mrs. Brownrigg considered, was carrying matters a little too far, but when she reflected on the characters of the other men in the village and on the condition in which the women almost invariably entered into the state of matrimony, she could not but esteem the uncompromising attitude he adopted. Even the vicar's gardener who grew the best lobelias in the county and took prizes at the local show with his tomatoes, suffered various lapses from virtue which the vicar had been forced diplomatically to ignore.

The amazing thing about Williams was his keen interest in nature. When she surprised him leaning thoughtfully on his spade, he always remarked that he was listening to the birds. Nothing seemed to give him more delight than their songs and he was apparently able to listen to them for hours on end. Sometimes he imitated their various calls for his admiring mistress and imparted small items of interest concerning their habits. 'In another walk of life,' Mrs. Brownrigg said, 'he would have been a great naturalist.'

Up to now Mrs. Brownrigg had never taken any great interest in nature, except of the human variety, but one day Williams dropped a remark which excited her curiosity. Remarking on the depredations committed by the bullfinches on the apple trees which for years he had neglected to prune, he mentioned the interesting fact that bullfinches are monogamous. Even more than that, they only mate once. This correspondence of natural and divine law moved Mrs. Brownrigg profoundly. Even at the cost of never eating an apple again she gave orders that they must never be chased from her garden which must be regarded from that time forth as a bullfinch sanctuary.

She enquired cautiously concerning the habits of other animals. She found that like human beings they varied and reflected that among them some had seen the light while others were still in pagan darkness. The sparrows in her ivy were a constant reminder of this, as they were so noisy in their activities she could not but be aware of their nefarious and unnatural practices.

From now on Mrs. Brownrigg courted Williams' company more than ever, and he, seeing in what direction the wind blew, supplied her with more and more information, often of a highly fictitious nature, concerning the wild life around her. When he was short of fact and hard pressed he drew on his fancy, knowing that no authority was greater than his own. In this way he came to describe rabbits as 'great family men' and earwigs as 'good mothers'.

But Mrs. Brownrigg was not the woman to stand and wonder. If a wrong needed righting, hers was the first voice raised, her hand the first on the plough. She had the true missionary spirit. She realized, of course, her limitations in this regard. She could neither praise nor blame, at least not in words understood by the animal world. Yet her spirit was not in any way downcast by this. Had not Saint Francis preached to the birds?

Reform, like charity, should begin at home. Next market day she set off, attended by a dumbfounded Williams, and bought thirty young cocks. They arrived towards evening, making a tremendous din, terrified and pecking savagely at one another. Triumphantly she headed the procession to the fowl run situated at the bottom of the garden and opening the gate shot them in, leaving the matter of selection to chance or nature.

Then next morning, when, full of hope, she went to see how they were getting on, a ghastly sight met her eyes. The fowl-run, strewn with corpses and feathers, resembled a battlefield. Two or three frightened cockerels who had survived the shambles were lurking, terrified and be-draggled, on the extreme tip of a small tree. They were too scared to make the slightest noise or even approach in the hope of food. The veteran rooster of the establishment was strutting up and down, his gills crimson with fury, crowing loudly, flashing his iridescent tail in the morning sunlight and showing off without shame. The hens were picking in-differently at their oats. Plainly the arrangement would not work.

For some days Williams was kept busy making small runs for the fowls. He grumbled savagely, but to no avail. His mistress drove him on tyrannically, never letting him rest. When he was finished each hen was isolated with a spouse. The apparent boredom of the newly wedded couples had no effect on Mrs. Brownrigg. She knew that with time they would accustom themselves to a life of marital virtue and make the best of it. She had seen many human couples forcibly united by her efforts with much the same look of bedraggled discontent, and knew that time cures all ills.

But Mrs. Brownrigg did not rest with putting her own house in order. She called a meeting at the school-house at which she delivered a lecture, worthy of Saint Francis, on her new mission — the bringing of light to the animal kingdom. She wished to form a committee but found a singular reluctance in others to join in her good work. The vicar called and tried to persuade her that animals had no souls, so their morals did not matter in the sight of the Almighty. She refuted him on every point. He went away puzzled and alarmed and confided in his wife that now Mrs. Brownrigg would probably leave her money to some crank society for the benefit of animals and not to the Church Fund or the Society for the Purification of the Young Person.

Now Mrs. Brownrigg began to go around the countryside preaching to the farmers. At first they listened to her with the kindly tolerance which all country people give to the slightly deranged. The state of the cows worried her. Was it not possible to provide a bull for each cow? She would help, of course. In language sufficiently obscure to be fit for a lady's ears they tried to wean her from the idea. Some indeed promised to consider the matter, hoping that she would go away and forget but here they were reckoning without their visitor. One farmer, indeed, went the length of assuring her that in future his bull calves would 'never be interfered with'.

Very soon the whole countryside was in an uproar. Farmers, irritated beyond endurance, could talk of nothing else when they met. Their wives were even more incensed, for they fancied they saw an attack on their own morals and decency. Their oversensitiveness in this regard led them to unparalleled impoliteness and more than once Mrs. Brownrigg was requested to take herself off. She left, her heart more bitter than ever against humanity.

The vicar became seriously worried. He discussed the question thoroughly with his wife. Mrs. Brownrigg's mania showed no signs of abating. Several interesting cases had turned up in the parish lately, which three months previously would have stirred her to instant action. Now the poor girls languished, without hope of rescue. Several cases of drunkenness had broken out which called for her active interference but she was deaf to all entreaties.

Then one evening a sad case was brought to the vicar's notice. He went down to the cottage and interviewed a weeping girl, a bewildered mother and an irate father. Finally after much persuasion, the girl, almost distracted by the storm of abuse and tears, gave in and named Mrs. Brownrigg's immaculate gardener as the cause of her downfall. The vicar could hardly believe his ears. He left the cottage hurriedly, uttering words of comfort and assurance. He must discuss the matter with his wife immediately.

They agreed that here they saw the finger of Providence. Truly He worked in a mysterious and often roundabout way. His wife urged the vicar to immediate action and, although late, she was sure that the importance of his news would excuse an untimely visit. She wrapped him up well, kissed him with unwonted affection and sent him on his way, if not exactly rejoicing, yet very well pleased.

The vicar panted up the hill to Mrs. Brownrigg's house, hurrying, hope in his breast. As he turned the corner and came in sight of it, a strange vision met his astonished eyes. He saw Mrs. Brownrigg, illuminated by the light of a torch, standing in the entrance gates in what looked like a nightgown, a long black scarf wound round her neck, a book in her hands, spectacles on her nose, reciting something. Her face, lit up with a beatific smile, was turned towards the fence. Full of curiosity he approached and was astonished to hear the familiar words of the Service for the Solemnization of Holy Matrimony. Even when he stood beside her she did not seem to notice him. Fascinated, he gazed into the ditch. Two small brown animals were romping and cavorting about in a suggestive manner. Any decent person would have turned aside and left them in peace. Not so Mrs. Brownrigg. She was consecrating the union of two hedgehogs. She finished, closed the book and turned towards the vicar, her face beaming. Then with a chuckle she said: 'The naughty fellow! He tried to marry someone else last night, but he got away before I could catch him. He's settled now.'

Without waiting for an answer, she turned towards the house, still chuckling, leaving the vicar staring after her, amazed and horrified, realizing that all was irretrievably lost.

The Wife's Petition

The lawyer rose slowly from his seat, cleared his throat, and tapped his papers lightly with a graceful white hand, on the little finger of which gleamed a signet ring. He was a handsome, middle-aged man, with a well-cut, expressionless face like the facade of a bank building. Raising his eyes to the judge, he said in a clear voice:

'My lud, this is a wife's petition.'

The judge did not appear to notice. He sat, almost immovable, in his chair, leaning slightly over his high desk, like a monk in meditation. His hooded eyes were like those of a vulture. On the rare occasions when he raised them they were as intent, as glittering and as hard as if indeed he were a bird of prey. His face was greyish-white, almost devoid of wrinkles, puffy, with eye-pouches. The corners of his mouth turned down. He did not appear to be paying the slightest attention to what was being said. He had already heard twenty cases that morning.

The lawyer continued reciting a formidable list of details. Listening to him one could not help but wonder how such a monster as the respondent could be allowed to inhabit the earth. The list was long, detailed, complete. The lawyer read it with feeling in his voice and certain dramatic pauses. But it was too much even for the judge. Fixing his shoe-button eyes on the barrister and waving a lazy, puffy hand, he made a noise, to those in court a quite incomprehensible noise, but the lawyer seemed to understand what he meant. So apparently did the usher. The barrister, after handing up some photographs, turned towards the end of the bench and with a gesture asked the petitioner to enter the witness-box.

Her elbow carefully held by an elderly solicitor's clerk with an evil leer in his eye, she stumbled forward, mounted the steps into the box and looked around her. She swayed slightly and held on to the edge of the witness-box with thin, white hands, the nails of which were painted bright scarlet.

The usher advanced towards her, handed her a Bible, and took up the printed oath which was lying on the edge of the box. He held it up before her and began to recite it. Holding the Bible aloft in a delicate wavering hand, she repeated the words after him in stifled tones, hesitating once or twice. When she had finished she looked around the court, first at the judge, then over the line of barristers and solicitors, finally letting her eyes rest on the people in the body of the court, most of them witnesses in other cases. Then her left hand made a feeble, fluttering gesture as if asking for help and the little solicitor's clerk, his back bent obsequiously from years of servitude, rushed forward with a chair. It was placed in the witness-box and she sat down.

She was a woman of uncertain age, a hard thirty or a well-preserved fifty. The only thing that betrayed her age was her hands, the long, thin, claw-like hands of an old woman. She was exquisitely dressed. Her fair hair, a little too fair, perhaps, curled softly from under her small black hat. Her face was most carefully made up, pale, but not too pale. The pallor was accentuated by the bright red of her thin lips. Over her eyes fell a small black veil. Her dress and furs were black and round her throat she wore a white ruffle. Altogether she gave the impression of a very smart French widow.

The barrister delayed a moment before questioning her. His glance was both apologetic and sympathetic. She swept the little veil back from her face and turned her eyes, dark with grief, towards the lawyer. In a soothing voice he asked, 'You are Mrs. Viola Clemency Arthurs?'

'I am.'

Her voice was low and deep.

'Please, address the judge,' said the lawyer.

She turned towards the judge and repeated: 'I am.'

The judge did not appear to hear. He sat, sphinx-like, gazing down at his folded hands.

'You reside at number 12, Elm Street, Mayfair?'

'I do.'

'You were married to the respondent, Walter Arthurs, on the 16th of April, 1927?'

She paused, then her voice came husky and vibrant. 'I was.'

The lawyer lowered his voice.

'Your marriage was happy at first, was it not?'

Another pause. Then the petitioner gathered herself together with an effort and with a tear-filled glance which swept the court and finally settled on the impassive face of the judge, a Buddha come to judgment, she replied slowly: 'Yes . . . very.'

Here the judge moved his head slightly. He unhooded one eye and looked at her. It would have been a comic gesture if the time, the place and the mood had been congenial. He lowered the eyelid again.

'Now, Mrs. Arthurs, on the 17th of March 1934, you became ill.'

'Yes, very ill. With neuritis. I was in frightful — '

'You went to a nursing-home, Mrs. Arthurs?' the barrister interrupted quickly.

'My husband put me in a nursing-home, yes.'

'How long were you there?'

'Six weeks.'

'And when you came out you noticed a change in your husband.'

Again the pause, again the anguished glance. 'A very great change.'

'Now, Mrs. Arthurs, please tell the court about this change, how it happened, how it manifested itself in his behaviour.'

A tiny handkerchief of delicate lace now appeared in her hand. She wafted it gently in the direction of her face but did not use it.

'He was — cold.'

At this point the judge again unsealed the shoe-button eye and looked at the petitioner. This time he looked a little longer. Then he closed it again.

'When were your suspicions first aroused?'

'I think I always knew.'

'But when had you any definite suspicions?'

'Nothing definite until my return from Egypt.'

'That was in February 1935.'

'Yes.'

'Why did you go to Egypt, Mrs. Arthurs?'

'My husband sent me there to visit my daughter by my first marriage.'

'Now what happened on your return?'

'My husband came to meet me and told me . . . the truth.'

'Did he mention the co-respondent's name?'

'He did.'

'What did he say?'

'He said . . . that he . . . wanted to marry . . . this woman . . . and asked me to set him free.'

'And what did you do?'

'I reasoned with him. I asked him not to forget . . . .'

'And what did he do?'

'He sent me to the West Indies.'

'You returned on August the 21st 1935?'

'Yes.'

'And when you got back, what happened?'

'He met me again . . . He told me . . . that if I entered the house . . . he'd go out.'

'What did you do then?'

Again the dark glance swept the court.

'I took a flat alone.'

'And then, Mrs. Arthurs, you got in touch with your solicitors.'

'I did.'

'Now, Mrs. Arthurs, would you mind identifying the photograph.'

The petitioner nodded.

The judge held out the photograph, the usher took it and brought it over to the witness-box.

Mrs. Arthurs looked at it and nodded again. Then turning to the judge, she said in a trembling voice, 'Yes, that is my husband.'

It was handed back to the judge, who now had a good look at it. He put it to one side with a grunt. The barrister nodded to the petitioner to get down. Gathering herself together, she lowered the little veil over her eyes and gave her hand to the obsequious little clerk who rushed forward and conducted her to a seat nearby. The chair was removed. The witness could stand.

The first witness was called. She was a young woman, very business-like in her manner and clipped in her speech. She was dressed quietly but expensively. She looked ill-tempered. Evidently she came very unwillingly.

'Your name is Winifred Brownlow?'

'Yes.'

'You are a married woman?'

'Yes.'

'You keep an apartment house at 14, Hunt Street, W.1.?'

'Yes.'

'A Mr. and Mrs. Arthurs took a flat in your house?'

'Yes, in September 1935. They stayed six months.'

'What accommodation did you provide in this flat?'

'There were two reception rooms, a bedroom, a dressing-room and a bath-room.'

'Was there a bed in the dressing-room?'

'Yes.'

'Was it used habitually?'

'I do not know. I never pried into their affairs in any way.'

'Did you notice anything . . . well . . . suspicious about them?'

'Why should I? They were charming people.'

'A different name on a letter? For example did any letters come addressed to a Mrs. Scott?'

'I do not inspect letters. I noticed nothing.'

'Will you please identify these photographs?'

The judge handed two photographs to the usher who brought them to the witness. She glanced at them disdainfully.

'Yes, these are photographs of the Mr. and Mrs. Arthurs who lived in my house.'

'Thank you, that will do.'

The witness got down without as much as a glance from the judge.

The next witness was a porter. He was very nervous. He

kept putting his hands in his pockets and taking them out
again, shifting his handkerchief from one pocket to another.
He gabbled the oath in a way which made one think that he
must be familiar with it. The barrister's tone was now sharp
and brisk.

'You are Charles Rae?'

'Yes, sir.'

'Kindly address the judge. You are employed at 14 Hunt
Street W.1. as porter-valet?'

'That's right.'

'You remember a Mr. and Mrs. Arthurs who came to live
there in September 1935?'

'That's right.'

'Did you notice anything suspicious about them — any
letters addressed to another name — any parcels?'

'Can't say as I did, sir.'

'You brought up the breakfast every morning?'

'That's right, sir.'

'Kindly address the judge.'

'Right you are, sir.'

'Did you notice anything when you brought up the breakfast in the morning?'

'Well — the lady was mostly in bed, but the gentleman
not.'

'Where was he?'

'In the bathroom or walking round the room.'

'Was he dressed?'

'Not as what you'd call dressed, sir.'

'He was in pyjamas?'

'That's right, sir.'

Here the judge waved his hand impatiently.

The witness stumbled down the steps of the witness-box,
wiping his forehead.

The judge lifted his eyelids and looking at the barrister,
uttered one word:

'Costs?'

'No, my lud,' answered the barrister.

The petitioner looked around, then turning to the little
clerk who sat by her side, she asked: 'Is that all?'

'Yes, indeed,' leering up into her face. 'He's knocking them off at a great rate this morning.'

The petitioner gathered her furs around her and moved slowly towards the door. Her tearful eyes swept the court for the last time. But no one was looking at her. Another barrister had risen to his feet, cleared his throat, tapped his papers and begun:

'This is a husband's petition, my lud.'

No Flowers

The lounge bar was almost empty when Jim Reade swung open the door to let Roma pass. Just two men at the far end were chatting casually to the bar-maid, who was busy polishing glasses and laying them, with a showy hand movement, upside down on the shelf, ready for the rush hour. Jim Reade took Roma confidentially by the elbow and bending slightly towards her, though she was tall, he piloted her to a table in the corner.

'This alright?' he asked.

'Fine.' She sat down on the creaking bent-wood chair and began to pull off her gloves. She had large, strong, capable hands, the nails unvarnished. She sat bolt upright, her shoulders straight, her head back.

'What will you have? A cocktail?'

'No thanks, a straight whisky.'

Jim Reade went to the bar and came back with the drinks.

'That's one thing I like about you, Roma, you take straight drinks. You're a man's woman.'

'Really, Jim, I'm surprised to hear it.'

She smiled and her lean face took on a gay charm, her dark eyes sparkled.

'Quite like old times, Roma. Having a drink here. It's a long time since we spent an evening together. Not since — well, not for a long time.'

'Quite a long time, now.'

'You look fine this evening.'

'Do I? That's good.'

'I'm so sorry, my dear, I forgot to bring you flowers. I

remembered that you used to like violets and I made a mental note and then the whole thing faded out of my mind.'

'Never mind. Forget again.'

'You know, Roma, I always say you're one of the best. The kind of pal a man likes to have around.'

'I know.' Roma smiled again.

'You don't believe it? Of course I do. You know I think a lot of you. I was only saying to Susan the other day that you were one of the best.'

'And what did Susan say?'

'She agreed. Susan thinks a lot of you, too.'

This time Roma laughed. She had a gay, pleasant laugh, whole-hearted and without a trace of malice. One of the men at the bar turned round and looked at her sharply and then passed some remark to his neighbour. They both laughed.

'Well, that's nice, Jim. I didn't think she'd even noticed me.'

'Yes, of course she did. You're worth noticing. She was saying, too, that you knew how to dress. That you had the good sense to stick to tailor-mades. They suit you.'

'Nice of her to notice. Tell me, Jim, why all this sudden attention. I'll buy it.'

Jim started and looked at Roma shrewdly.

'So you don't think I really mean all this. Honest, I mean every word I say.'

'Well, that's fine!' There was something light, something incredulous in the tone of her voice.

'Don't you believe me? Don't you think that sometimes a man likes to take an intelligent woman to dinner, a thoughtful woman. That's the word, thoughtful.'

'I see.'

'Hasn't anyone ever told you that you were a damned intelligent woman?'

'Oh, lots.'

'There you are. You see. I know Susan's a sweet kid, easy on the eye and all that. But sometimes a bit heavy on the hand, you know. Though mind you, I'm saying nothing against Susan. I'm very fond of Susan. In my own way, I suppose I'm in love with Susan. But sometimes a man likes to spend an evening with a sensible woman who can talk, discuss things.'

'Can't you discuss things with Susan?'

'Go on, Roma. Stop ragging.'

'But I'm not. I've always wondered what girls like Susan do talk about when they're with men. I don't know.'

'Oh nothing, you know. Just the usual things like "Let's have a drink" or "Let's go to the pictures," or "Let's pick up the Mannings and go out somewhere". You know.'

'Sounds interesting.'

'What do they talk to you about?'

'To me? Oh, the Susans of this world pass me by. If they do notice me it is for one of three reasons; to complain of the Jims of this world, and they generally have reason; to borrow a little money to tide over between Jims or to get the address . . . of a dressmaker. I myself go to a tailor, but I keep the address handy. When their particular trouble is all fixed up, I know them no more.'

'Now that's why it's so pleasant to spend an evening with you. You're so sensible, so intelligent.'

'I seem to have heard that somewhere before.'

'But it's true. That's what I mean, it's true. You are. You can talk to a man without any nonsense and he can say what's on his mind. You're a tonic. That's the word, tonic.'

'Since you don't need money, or a dressmaker, I suppose what you want is advice.'

'Ah, stop ragging, Roma. But honestly, what would you do in my place?'

'How?'

'About Susan.'

'You haven't explained yet, Jim. Do you want me to tell you how to get rid of her with the least amount of trouble to yourself, or how to get her to change her way of life? You're much more of an expert on these matters than I am.'

'It isn't that. It's that Susan has thrown up her job.'

'Thrown up her job? Why? Are you going to be married or what?'

'No — no. It's like this. She's thrown up her job and here I am and I don't know what to do.'

'Quite easy. She'll get another.'

'Not so easy, Roma. And it was a mean trick. Definitely

mean. That's what I feel.'

'But surely she has a right to throw up her job if she wants to? I've thrown up half a dozen or so in my time.'

'Oh, you. You're different. You've always been an independent woman. You've never bothered anyone. I mean, you've always done things on your own responsibility. That's the word. Responsibility.'

'What you're trying to tell me is that Susan has thrown up her job on someone else's responsibility. Yours, I suppose?'

'Ex-act-ly.' He leaned forward and his handsome face looked fish-like in its intensity.

'How, if I may ask?'

'Well, there she was, grousing around, complaining about this and that and about how the old Madame drove her and treated her like a dog. And how she was blamed for ink being on a new model and what not. "Well, why don't you chuck it?" I said, thinking that would settle her. But believe me, the very next day, she gave in her notice.'

'And then . . .?'

'Then she ups and says I told her to. And now what am I to do? Honest, Roma, you know me. I don't grudge the money. If she needs it, she can have it. It's the slyness of the thing that gets me. Hurling herself on my neck like that.'

'Oh well, it's a man's world and you must take the consequences.'

'It *is* mean. It's underhand. That's the word. Underhand. I feel stung.'

'It won't break you. There's lots of jobs for a goodlooking girl like Susan. Tell her she can't lie down on you, give her five pounds and send her out to look for a job. That's my advice, for what it's worth.'

'I can't do that, Roma. It looks so bad.'

'If you want to find some way of making a nasty deal look like open-handed generosity, you've come to the wrong shop this time.'

'Joking apart, Roma. What's the best thing to do?'

'I'm telling you, Jim. Just plain, straight talking.'

Jim Reade wriggled uncomfortably. The bent-wood chair creaked under his embarrassment.

'You're a good sort, Roma. Haven't I always said you were

the best pal a man could have? Pal, that's the word. That's you. Mind you, I'm fond of Susan. Don't think that I'm not. Now suppose you were to ask Susan out and explain.'

Roma began to laugh. Her laughter came in little gurgles, like water over stones. Jim Reade became more and more embarrassed and the chair creaked wildly in sympathy. The men and the barmaid looked at the couple in the corner, turned away again, nodded and exchanged looks.

'Jim Reade, you have a neck. You have.'

'Ah, stop ragging, Roma. This is serious.'

Roma stretched out her hand for her gloves.

'I'll drop her a hint, Jim, for her sake. Not for yours. For I know what you'll do if I don't.'

'How? What?'

'Drift away, my gallant knight, like an autumn leaf before the wind.'

'Now, Roma, you don't mean . . . .'

'I mean every word of it. I haven't forgotten, Jim, I'm sick of silly men. I'm sick of being treated like a cushion on which to lay their weary heads, or a handkerchief into which they can weep their silly tears. I'm bored with their troubles which they're too cowardly to face. I'm tired of being a good sort, and sensible and intelligent. And I'm hungry, ravenous. I want a steak, a large steak. Do you hear, I'm hungry.'

Jim Reade looked at his watch.

'I'm so sorry, dear. Forgive me. I never noticed that the time was getting on. We'll go right away.'

The door of the saloon bar opened and several men forced their way in together, talking and laughing. The bar-maid smiled and reached for the glasses.

'Good evening, Mr. Smith. And Mr. Richards. Pleasant evening. Lovely weather we're having for the time of year.'

Roma watched them pass, almost sadly.

'And do me the favour, Jim, of keeping the conversation impersonal. Racing. I respect your opinion on horses.'

'And remind me, Roma, to buy you some flowers.'

It's in the Bag

He was only half listening to what the two other fellows were saying. Mostly stable-talk anyway and he was heart sick of that. God! Would they never let up on their everlasting gabble — horses, weights, lengths, stewards, owners, trainers — round and round like the old horse in the pound. He was looking over Ned Sheridan's shoulder at the far corner of the lounge. He was watching her as she listened to a tall red-headed man. She wasn't saying much herself, just listening and looking round, sharply eyeing everyone that passed in and out of the room. He watched her pull a piece of woollen thread from the inside of her pocket, slowly roll it into a ball between her hands and pop it swiftly, almost furtively, into her mouth.

She didn't seem to be paying much attention to the red-headed fellow's talk either. He was mad about something and no mistake. Anybody could see that from the way his forehead was puckered up and the fierce look in his eyes. God! And he was red about the gills. And the way he kept pounding the table with the flat of his hand.

'You're kinda absent-minded, Joe,' said Ned Sheridan suddenly. 'What's atin' ye?'

'Nothin',' said Joe. He nodded towards the corner where the girl was sitting and asked: 'Do yez happen to know who's that jane over there?'

Ned Sheridan twisted round his neck and had a good look.

'Sure. That's Mrs. Fenwick, Harry Fenwick's wife. That's him there givin' out to her now. By the looks of it, if he had a drop more liquor inside of him, he'd likely be doin' more than talkin'. 'Twouldn't be the first time the same lady sported a black eye.'

'And small blame to him from what I hear tell.' added Matt Riordan. 'Ye know him surely, Joe. He's a place down in Carlow and a string of broken-kneed nags. Ruined himself backin' his own horses.'

'Sure,' said Joe. 'So that's the fella.'

Matt Riordan leaned forward and spoke in a loud, hoarse whisper: 'They do say that she's been doin' a line wi' Alec Watson, the bookie.'

'Fenwick ud have his work cut out for him to blacken that boyo's eye,' said Ned Sheridan with a grin. 'I think little the worse of him for that. I wouldn't like to take on the same myself.'

'What drew yer eye, Joe?' asked Matt.

'She came up and spoke to me at the Park today.'

'What did she want?'

'She asked me was I tryin'?'

'And you said?'

'I said: "Lady, I'm always tryin'?" Just like that.'

Joe jerked back his head and winked. Ned Sheridan's monkey face twisted into a grin and he winked at Matt Riordan with a sideways nod of his head.

'And where was the wife, Joe, to let ye be assaulted by an unknown female in a public place?'

'She wouldn't show her face,' said Joe. 'Just had her teeth out.'

'That ull mean a few weeks' grace for you,' said Matt.

'Dunno about that. She'll soon get used to herself again.'

'Well, I'd best be goin',' said Ned Sheridan. He rose, lifted his raincoat from the back of the chair and settled his hat carefully on his head. 'So long boys. See ye tomorra.'

'Hold yer hurry, Ned,' said Matt. 'I'll be along.'

Joe watched them push their way through the tables and sidle across to the door. Then he looked over to the corner where the girl was sitting. She was alone now. She was leaning back against the green velvet of the wall-couch, coolly examining each person who entered or left the room. Her dark eyes betrayed no curiosity. They just looked and looked away. Her jaws moved slowly as she chewed the piece of wool. Was she waiting for anyone, he wondered. For her husband? For that big bruiser, Alec Watson?

Suddenly she looked over at him and smiled. He had been waiting for this, hoping for it. He got up and crossed the room with the slow, bandy, knee-jerking walk of the jockey, letting his weight fall on the sides of his shoes. She did not look at him when he sat down beside her. As he looked at her he groped to find some clever phrase, even some word which would turn her attention towards him. But only the most banal words came to his mind, vulgar, cheap words, contradicting by their very sound the fever in his veins.

'How's tricks?' he asked.

'Fine! How's yours?' Her voice was low, hoarse and even.

'What are ye havin'?'

'Double Scotch.'

He called the waiter and gave the order. 'Waitin' for someone?'

'No one in particular.' She smiled. He could see the blue wool between her teeth.

'Say, if ye're hungry, have a sanwidge.'

She laughed and shook her head.

'What do you do it for?'

'Dunno. I like it. I eat the inside out of all my pockets.'

'And other fellas', too, I'll bettya.'

Again she laughed. 'What do you want to know for?'

'I have me reasons.'

'Is that all you have?' she asked slyly.

The directness of the question set him back on his rockers. He swallowed his drink and then smiled with self-satisfaction. He could feel himself rising to the fence, easily, beautifully. 'Tell me now,' he asked in a wheedling voice. 'Why did ye speak to me in the paddock?'

She turned a simple guileless look upon him. 'Because I wanted to know what would win the three o'clock race.'

This wasn't the answer he had expected but he tried again. 'But why me? Why not one of the other fellas?'

'You'd no peroxide following you.'

The eager smiles were wiped from his face. He looked angry, disappointed and hungry. The girl studied the crest-fallen face and then smiled in a soft, kind way. 'You rode well,' she said.

To all men who live in the public eye, praise is as dew to the thirsty earth. His wrinkled, leathery face smiled again. 'Not so bad,' he said.

'Not so bad!' The girl's brown eyes opened wide in astonishment. 'I thought it was marvellous. The way you drew your mount out just at the right moment. I've never seen better.'

'Do you say so now?' A warm glow spread over his body. His hands tingled. He bent forward and seized the girl's knee. To his surprise she pressed the fingers hard between the bones of her knees. But there was no change of face. She remained aloof, kind, smiling. At the same time she drew a string of wool from the inside of her pocket, rolled it between her palms and pushed it between her teeth. Joe drew away his hand.

'Aw, spit it out,' he said.

'Got anything for tomorrow?' The girl asked.

'Sure. Dead cert.'

'No kidding?'

'Not a word of a lie. And starting at ten to one.'

'Go on!'

'It's in the bag.'

'Nothing's in the bag till the flag goes up.'

'That's God's truth mostly. But this is in the bag alright. Nothin' to beat it.'

The girl's eyes, unflinching, shuttered, looked into his. For a moment he hesitated and then chanced his arm. 'I've a room upstairs,' he said.

'Interesting,' she murmured.

'I can't go shouting any horse's name down here,' he said peevishly. 'Anyone might hear.'

'You can write it down. I've learned to read.' Her knee pressed gently against his, giving him courage.

'It's quiet there,' he said. 'We could have a drink and a talk.'

She looked at him sharply and then looked away. 'I'll follow you out,' she murmured.

In the hall he ran into Mrs. Tracy, the manageress, a fat, red-faced woman who looked as if she were going to burst her stays with every breath she drew.

'Oh, Mr. Morris, I'm so sorry,' she gasped. 'I thought you had left with Mr. Sheridan. Mrs. Morris has just rung up to know where you were.'

'That's alright, Mrs. Tracy. I'll give her a ring later on myself. Look, can ye send a bottle of Haig and two glasses up to number four. I've some business to talk over with a lady. Matter of a mount.'

'I'll send Mick up right away. Anything good for tomorrow?'

'Nothin'. But ye can ask Ned Sheridan. He may be on to something.'

The girl sat on the edge of the bed and looked around the room, just as if it were the first time she had ever seen such a room. There was nothing strange or queer about it. It was like every other room of its sort from Malin Head to Mizen Head. The same pink roses on the wallpaper, on the water-jug, on the counterpane and if you took the trouble to look hard you'd find them in the dinginess of the carpet itself. The same dusty lace curtains covered the window. The same grimy feel where you put down your hand.

She took the glass Joe handed to her, sipped, placed it on the floor at her feet and went on studying the wallpaper. Joe didn't sit down. He stood on the ragged hearth-rug, balancing himself on the sides of his feet.

'Well!' he said.

The girl looked at him, smiled and repeated: 'Well!'

'What do you say about it?' he asked. His face was the carved face of an idol.

'We were talking about a horse,' said the girl.

'We were, girleen. I was to give ye a horse. Well, and so I will.'

He came towards her and caught her knee. Again the answering pressure. Again the secret, dark, aloof smile. His eyes went misty.

'It's in the bag, you say?'

'Sure, girleen, it's in the bag.' Should he tell her now? If he did, she might just say thank ye and leave. If he didn't she mightn't believe him and leave without a thank ye. He began to pace restlessly up and down the room. Suddenly he stopped dead and said:

'Crazy Jane. Four o'clock.'

'Thanks,' said the girl. She did not move. His heart rose.

'Ye can put yer shirt on it.'

The girl looked up sadly and stretched out her hands.

'But I haven't got a shirt.'

'Well, yer shift then.'

'Nothing. I haven't a penny to put on.' She laughed a low, hoarse, cackling laugh.

Joe eyed her suspiciously. What was the game? Trying to back out now and go and tell her pals? Tell that big bruiser, Alec Watson? He'd pay well for the information. Was she trying to force him to back it for her? God, he was a fool and no mistake. He shouldn't have told her, not yet. He caught her by the shoulder and tried to force her back. But he never as much as rocked her base. She was strong and heavy. His muscles were not pushing muscles, but the muscles a fly has, for holding on, clinging, pulling. He couldn't push a wheel-cart over, let alone a great mare like this one.

Furious, he walked across the room and looked down through the dingy window on the busy street below. He tried to bring back calm and reason to his mind by forcing it to notice what was going on down there, the people going in and out of the church across the way, the people walking along the pavement, some hurrying, some taking their time. The carts. The lorries. The trams. By the time he had counted six trams and repeated their numbers he was seized by a great fear that she had vanished. But when he turned round she was still there, rolling a piece of woollen thread between her palms. As he moved away from the window, his foot kicked against the slop-pail.

In a frenzy of rage he unfastened his trousers and made water into the bucket. The girl watched him, her mouth turning up with amusement. 'Little gentleman!' she murmured.

Then he stood over her again, shook her shoulder and shouted. 'But it's in the bag, I tell ye.'

The girl held out one hand and gently rubbed the palm with the fingers of the other. The brown eyes, smiling, relentless, looked into his. Anger swelled his brain, beat against

his starting eyeballs. Crouching in front of her, pressing his
bandy knee-bones one against the other, rocking lightly, he
banged his thigh with his fist and shouted: 'I tell ya, it's in
the bag. Any girl ud be glad of a straight tip like that. What
do ye take me for? God Almighty! Do ye think ye can make
a hare outa me?'

He stopped suddenly, straightened and listened. His eyes
moved unsteadily from the girl on the bed to the door. His
quick ear had caught the tap of a high-heeled step on the
passage. Then Mrs. Tracy's voice, panting, agitated.

'Now Mrs. Morris, now me dear, come along down to the
office where it's warm. Ye'll get yer death up here in the
cold. Sure amn't I tellin' ye that he left an hour ago wit'
Mr. Sheridan. Didn't I see him go wit' me own eyes.'

There was a hissing and the word 'Liar!'

'Now Mrs. Morris, I warn ye. I won't have any rows in this
hotel. It's a decent place and I'll have no scandal.'

Joe took up his stand in the middle of the room, facing
the door. He glowered fiercely as he watched the furious
rattling of the door-handle.

'It's open,' he said.

The door was flung open but the woman who opened it
backed away from the light into the darkness of the passage.
She gave a muffled scream from behind her hands.

'Well!' said Joe, making no move.

'The peroxide has caught you up,' said the girl on the bed.

'Hell blast yer sowl,' said Joe quietly.

'Keep yer bad language to yerself, Joe Morris,' hissed the
woman in the passage. 'And come along out. I've somethin'
to say to ye. And you! Haven't you a man of yer own?'

'Come along in and say it,' said the girl. 'I'd like to hear it
for myself.'

'She can't,' said Joe. 'She's had her teeth out.'

A muffled scream from the woman in the passage and
more muttered threats.

'Well,' said the girl on the bed. 'I think we've settled our
business. There's no use hanging about and getting in the
way. I'll just say goodbye and toddle off.'

Joe watched her push her handbag firmly under her arm,
brush the front of her coat, touch her back hair and then

walk slowly from the room, past the muttering peroxide-headed woman who held her hands over her mouth, past the fat panting Mrs. Tracy who strained her stays at every breath. He could hear her slow steps as she walked down the corridor.

Joe never moved. He never as much as turned his head to look at the screaming woman who threw herself across the bed. He stood looking out into the passage, his face grey beneath the tan, the wrinkles round his eyes showing white. He put out his hand and groped for his glass. It rattled against his teeth and when he tipped it back he found it was empty.

The Death of my Father

The door opened and the Curé entered the bare, little parlour. I had been wandering restlessly round the room, looking first out of the window that faced the narrow, noisy street and then through the french window that opened on to a small cobbled courtyard, edged with flowers. The room, with its bare, white-washed walls and stiff hard chairs ranged in a row around it, did not bear looking at. It spoke too clearly of the life of a celibate. But the little garden showed a hand as tender and gentle as any woman's. Flowers grow best when a loving hand has planted them.

I looked curiously at the priest, at this man who loved flowers. He was fifty or so, a tall, thick-set Norman, probably the son of some rich farmer. He had the hard features and the strong, broad hands of those who till the soil. The soutane hung awkwardly on his clumsy body and his large feet, in heavy boots, stuck out rebelliously from beneath the hem. He did not look at me, just stood silently in the doorway, his eyes towards the ground. I could not help thinking that it had not been easy for this man to become a priest.

'I have come in answer to your telegram, Monsieur le Curé,' I said. 'I am sorry I could not come immediately. I was out of town. My father is ill?'

The Curé now looked at me. His eyes were friendly — light-blue Norman eyes, with their hint of child-like cunning.

'I regret, Madame,' he began and then, having cleared his throat nervously, continued: 'Your father, the good God has called him home.'

If he had feared an outburst of grief, he must have been

relieved. I felt no grief and I could not simulate what I did not feel. My father could be no more dead to me today than he had ever been. What he had once been still lived in me.

'I knew it.'

'Ah,' said the priest, 'God has His ways of helping us all. I was afraid it might be a shock.'

'No. I always know when those who belong to me die. And, too, I have not seen him for years. There were family troubles.'

The Curé shook his head as if these were of little account.

'A good man,' he said. His eyes now looked intently into mine. From the tone of his voice I could see that he had loved my father. 'A good and just man. God's fires burned fiercely in his soul. He mortified himself before God.'

I could not help thinking with a certain bitterness that all who knew him, my mother, his family, myself, would have been happier if he had mortified himself before men. God is the refuge of the proud man who cannot bear the burden of his guilt towards his fellows.

'I knew him,' I replied coldly. 'When did he die?'

'On Monday evening. We buried him here this morning. If I had known I would have waited for you.' He spread out his large, strong hands in apology. 'But you see, Madame, I did not know.'

'It is better as it is.' I was thankful to be spared. I had once, as a child, sneaked into a graveyeard during a funeral and heard the thud of earth on the coffin.

I went towards the door and then hesitated. I was moved by a sudden, intense curiosity.

'I must thank you, mon père, for your kindness to my father. If it is not too much trouble, I should like to see where he lived.'

'If Madame will allow me to accompany her.'

We left the presbytery together. The strong sunlight hit me between the eyes, blinding me after the shaded room. The street, cobbled in flint, the flint walls of the houses caught the heat and radiated it in all directions. I could feel the sudden perspiration start out on my body.

'Fait b'en chaud,' I said.

The Curé smiled. Here in the open street he again turned

away his eyes.

'It will ripen the harvest,' he replied.

We walked along together, but apart. As if fearful of the eyes of men, he kept his distance, stepping out a pace or two in front of me. He did not offer to speak to me but I scarcely noticed.

I was thinking how strange it was that my father, with all the world before him, should settle in this little French town where he had sent me to school. What impulse had driven him here, to end his days among strangers? I tried to imagine him walking through these flint-paved streets, beneath these old Roman walls. I tried to imagine him speaking to the people in his strange stiff French and I could not. I could only remember him, broad-shouldered and strong, as he walked through the paddock at home, flicking off the heads of the tall daisies with his riding-crop.

'The town hasn't changed much,' I said to the Curé. 'I used to go to school here.'

'I wondered how a foreign lady came to speak with a good Norman accent,' he replied without looking round.

We turned into a gateway and crossed a courtyard. In the middle of the yard, the priest threw back his head with an abrupt gesture and looking up at one of the windows, called out, 'Madame Herpin! Madame Herpin!'

A head appeared at a second storey window, a brown face with steady, sharp, black eyes, a high, narrow forehead crowned by a roll of dyed black hair. In spite of the heat, the woman was wearing a knitted spencer over her black alpaca dress.

'Monsieur le Curé?'

'Your pardon for disturbing you, Madame. Could you throw down the keys of Monsieur Delahaie's house? His daughter is just arrived from Ireland.'

The head disappeared and in a moment returned. With a snake-like movement a hand darted through the open window and the keys fell on the stones at our feet. The priest picked them up. The head did not disappear again. Instead it was joined by another, dark too and younger but just as hard and ugly. The two pairs of black eyes looked at me, examining my face, my clothes, my shoes. They weighed me up, considered me, reduced me to francs and sous. Did these harpies attend to the wants of a dying man, of my father who hated ugly women?

The lower half of the house in which my father had lived was closed. He had only used the two upper rooms. We mounted the crooked steps. The priest opened the door of the sitting-room and I entered.

The room was poorly furnished but neat and clean. A table and a chair stood beside the window; a wooden armchair near the fireplace; a shelf of books; a small desk; behind a curtain some simple kitchen utensils. Against a wall a wooden bench and on it a hard pillow. What nights of penance had he passed there? Remembering the violence of his nature, I shuddered.

I turned towards the bookshelf. Some of the books I knew already. There was the well-read *Life of Napoleon*. He had a great admiration of Napoleon. There was Kant and Spinoza, Thomas à Kempis, Bossuet, Lamartine, some volumes of Hugo and Shakespeare's tragedies; many minor works on theology. In the corner a small book I had once given him, *Moby Dick*. I took it down and opened it. There, across the flyleaf, written in a childish hand with which I was no longer familiar, I read: "To my dear Father, Martin-Eustace Delahaie, from his loving daughter, Anne-Louise." Then the date: 14th May, 1913. We each brought my father a present on his birthday and kissed his leathery, brown cheek. Then again at Christmas. The only times we ever kissed him.

The priest stood with his back to the empty fireplace and watched me with a sharp penetrating glance as I searched. What was I searching for? I did not know. I opened the desk. A pile of bills, paid and receipted, lay in one corner. Some business letters. A bank passbook. Writing materials. Nothing of a personal nature. As I glanced through the letters, I remarked:

'He was an orderly man, my father.'

The priest sighed.

'He wished always to arrange, fix, make sure. He would have tried to make a quicksand firm.'

In a drawer of the desk I discovered a couple of pamphlets which I turned over casually at first. They were my own early

work — "On the use of the preterite subjunctive in Old
Provençal ?' and "On the origin of the 5,5 hexameter in
French". Also the text of an old Venetian poem, given and
inscribed to me by the commentator, Mario Esposito. Why
had he kept these relics of a past life? He could not have
understood a word of them. They were as technical as a
treatise on engineering. I turned over the pages of the paper
on metrics and came across the lines, heavily underlined:
"Mais ton coeur est traître et ta bouche ment".

Father! Whose heart? Yours, mine or another's?

There was no photograph of me in the room, nor of any
of us. Only an old book and these scholastic papers. I rolled
them up and put them under my arm.

One day he had taken me out for a riding lesson. When I saw
my father's great black hunter, prancing restlessly like a
dancer, and held by the groom, I backed away in fear. My
father touched me on the shoulder.

'Come here,' he said sharply.

He held out his hand to help me mount. I looked at the
nervous animal, at his flat ears and rolling eyes, at the dark
sweat of his flanks. As I placed my hands on the saddle and
my foot in my father's hand, I turned round with unaccustomed courage: 'Must I, Father?'

'Up!' said my father. I was in the saddle. Mike, the groom,
let go the bridle and I was off, down the paddock to where
a low hedge with a deep ditch waited for me. The hedge rose
before me and then came towards me. The horse had stopped
dead and thrown me out over his ears. As I lay in the ditch I
realized that my father had known what would happen. This
was to teach me to keep a firm seat. He picked me up and
insisted that I should mount again. I shook my head and
burst into tears. My left arm hung limply by my side. The
collar-bone was broken.

'God!' he shouted in disgust. 'What it is to be surrounded
by women. Get along to your mother.'

A week later the horse killed the groom.

He tried to teach me to swim. He threw me into the river
and let me get myself out. Then threw me in again. I was

always a poor horsewoman and a bad swimmer.

Everything he tried to teach me, I failed at. He had begun to regard me as a failure. My taste for scholarship came as a surprise to him, but even there I could only work at the subjects he despised or could not understand. Then, suddenly, he became intensely proud of me and, to encourage me, forbade every distraction.

I saw my father only once after my marriage. I thought then that he had disapproved because he thought I had married badly. But no, he would have objected, no matter whom I had married.

I went home because my mother was ill. At that time I was pregnant. No one had told my father, it seemed. I did not blame my mother. I knew my father well enough to realize how difficult it was to speak to him on such matters. He came into my mother's bedroom where I was sitting. When I rose from the chair to come towards him, he looked at me. His dark eyes distended and his upper lip set hard over his teeth. The words were choked in his throat. He stared at me for a moment, at my distorted body, and then turned on his heel and left the room. I felt the blood rise to my head with anger and shame. I turned towards my mother.

'Child, do not mind him,' she said with unusual kindness. 'He is a strange man.'

I left the house half an hour later. I could not stay there. As I walked to the railway station I felt as if all mankind were pointing at me, jeering at me. I felt ugly and ashamed of my ugliness. When I got home, I sat in the corner of my couch, wrapped in a shawl and snapped at all who came near me. Since that day I am moved at the sight of a pregnant woman, it arouses such pity and anguish of memory in my heart.

Six months later, my father became a Catholic, settled some money on his family and went away.

I turned to the priest.

'Was my father alone when he died?' I asked. 'Was there no woman with him?'

The priest misunderstood my meaning.

'Rest assured, Madame. There was never any scandal attached to your father's name. He was a saint.'

He opened the bedroom door with a gesture, as if to bear out his words. I looked in. I saw my father's dressing-gown on the back of a chair, his razor-strop hanging from the door-handle. The narrow pallet-bed was covered with a sheet. Beneath that sheet he had slept and died.

'Was he alone?'

'No, Madame. I was there and the doctor. He was a strong man and death came hard. He cried out in his agony, setting his will against God's.'

'What did he die of?'

'Of blood-poisoning, Madame.'

His blood had been poisoned long before, I thought. He had drunk it in with his mother's milk.

'Why did he wish to see me?' I asked. 'He had not seen me for many years.'

'He wished to show you the way to God.'

'Had he found it?' I asked, my voice now harsh with anger. The Curé spread out his large hands.

'Let us hope,' he answered.

'The way to God, mon père, each man must find for himself.'

'For us, there is only one way. Your father suffered, knowing you had turned from it. He cried out to God for you. He wanted you to find happiness in God.'

'No man or woman has any right to happiness in this world in which we live. I doubt if we have any right even to wish for it.'

The priest shook his head and closed the bedroom door.

'You would like to see his grave?' he asked.

I remembered the horror of a French cemetery. I could see the beaded garlands, the wreaths of *immortelles,* the shabby economy of the French even in death. I could see the newly turned earth. No. What matter where a man's bones are laid?

'I shall see a notary about the disposal of my father's property,' I said harshly. Resentment against this priest was growing in me, resentment against all priests for their stupid assurance. 'I must thank you again for your kindness to my father. I hope you will accept some money for the poor of your parish.'

The priest smiled at my anger. My rude words did not offend him. He was accustomed to read the human heart. And he knew my father, that proud, arrogant man, only humble before God.

'Would you wish to have a mass said for the repose of his soul?'

'His soul? My father's soul? Let it meet its creator naked! No, nothing! I'll send you some money but not for that.'

The priest continued to smile and followed me down the stairs. In the lower doorway, I turned and held out my hand. He barely touched the fingers.

'Goodbye, mon père. And many thanks.'

'Your father,' said the priest in a gentle voice. 'He died at peace. Though at first he struggled, was resentful of death. But he submitted his will to the will of God when I touched him with the holy oil. Then his soul was at peace.'

I left the priest. I could not utter another word. I could see him as he bent over my father. I could see those strong hands touch my father's eyes, his lips, the palms of his hands, the soles of his feet.

Eyes that had strayed through desire, lips that had strayed through lust, hands that had strayed through touch, feet that had wandered.

Men are never God's creatures

You could watch him with delight as he walked up the hill to the paddock beyond the village where he kept his horses. For he had the beautiful artless walk of a man whose whole body acted in concert, whose muscles lay easily on his bones; the quick, light step; the long, slenderly boned legs; the narrow waist and hips; the flat, wide-shouldered back; the arms overlong. As you watched him, you would think that Almighty God had, for once, created the perfect man.

Yet when Jerry MacAvoy turned round and you saw the faint melancholy of his light blue eyes, you could not help but laugh. With that sardonic humour of which He alone is capable, the Creator had clapped on him the face of the clown; that face with the large gashed mouth, the small, separated teeth, the widely spaced round eyes, the bulbous nose and harsh colour which from the earliest ages has moved men to irrepressible mirth. Its bare melancholy creates no answering melancholy. Its tragedy must be borne alone.

Perhaps in compensation, as is so often the case, his nature bore out the semi-divine mask. Of an evening, in Delahunty's bar, he was the best possible company. The men who gathered there listened with shining eyes to his shrewd wit, his ready answers and laughed with loosened girth. They savoured their drink the better for his company, their blood flowed more easily, the lurking, dark shadows of their minds dissolved. They carried home to their gloomy houses, to their too familiar beds, something of the poetry of his humour.

He was lucky, too, in his wife, Anna, a lighthearted girl who could forget the comedy of his face in the delight of his body, and knew that no other woman ever would. With happiness in her heart she left him free and attended to the humdrum business of the butcher's shop. He liked his glass, he liked to dance, he liked a pretty girl as well as another, but her only rival was the mare, Janetta.

It was his custom when he attended the markets to buy cattle, to keep his eyes open for some likely young horse to break and train and then sell to some English visitor over for the hunting. In this way he found Janetta. She was younger than he would have liked. She had not yet lost the furry tail nor the coltish movements of extreme youth. But something in the way she nuzzled up to him, nipped his sleeve and then started away, attracted him. Indeed she never quite lost this coltishness, even when she put on strength and beauty.

When he went to the paddock and called her, she would come running, only to stop dead just beyond the reach of his outstretched hand. Then, skittishly, she would toss her mane, flatten her ears in pretended anger, sidestep and circle around him while he coaxed, wheedled and called her endearing names. 'Hey, Janetta! Come here, ye beauty, ye darlin', ye lovely whoore!'

It was no use. She never answered his pleading. Only when he turned his back on her and walked towards the gate, she followed, her soft nose nibbling his coat, her hot breath on his neck.

But when he threw his leg across her back, he was her master: when his long thighs clipped her sides, she was docile and quiet. Her body answered every movement of his, was of one rhythm with his. No other horse had given him such pleasure; no other horse ever made him feel so much a man.

Then he would slap her with the flat of his hand and shout to her and though the words he spoke were the same, they were no longer pleading, no longer coaxing, but strong, triumphant: 'Yup, Janetta! Up, girleen! Up, my lovely whoore!'

She had one bad fault. It arose indeed from her very strength, her lightness, her skittishness. She flew her banks. And this in the Irish countryside, with its sunk ditches and uneven levels, is not only a bad fault, but a dangerous one. It took Jerry a long time to cure her. He raised the bank in the paddock until he forced her to alight and change her feet. He drove her close into ditches before he let her rise. At last it seemed that she was cured.

A new curate came to the village. He arrived in a fine new motor-car, a present from an adoring mother, a well-to-do widow who owned a grocery store and public house in the next county. The women liked young Father Tracy, for his youth, for his holy air which was nothing more than a fixed stare, and for the wild sermons he preached condemning sin. Father Mooney, the parish priest, now falling into years, had almost ceased to worry about sin, taken up as he was with his ageing digestion. Hardly a Sunday passed now without Father Tracy showing them, in all its allure, the rosy path to Hell. Dances without proper supervision of the clergy, drink, cards, horse-racing, women's clothes and illicit love-making, all came under the scourge of his tongue. They trembled while they listened. So near they were to losing their immortal souls.

The men said nothing one way or another until Father Tracy asked for 'oat-money'. The parish was a large one. It straggled up the glen and over the mountainside. The former curate had gone around it on an old nag. Once a year he had asked for contributions of oats or money to feed the horse. Those who had oats sent a bag and those who had none gave a little money, according to their means. Willingly given since the priest was poor. And now here was Father Tracy asking for 'oat-money' to buy petrol for his car.

The men discussed the matter in Delahunty's bar. The general opinion was that it was nothing more than a piece of impertinence to ask for 'oat-money' for a car.

'Ah, he's greedy,' said Jerry. 'And greed in man or beast is deplorable. It makes for a big belly and no staying power.'

'He's young and strong, let him walk,' shouted the Growler, a large, ferocious man who prided himself on his scholarship. 'Let him practise Christian humility and walk.'

'God save ye!' said Jerry. 'How could the likes of him walk? Barrin' the disgrace of puttin' one foot in front of the other in the sight of his parishioners, the man's bad on his feet. He'd likely fall down and break his knees.'

'Ye take it too lightly, Jerry,' shouted the Growler again. 'Far in a way too lightly. Here he comes to this place and from the talk he lets out of him, ye'd think he'd landed in Sodom and Gomorrah. Ye'd think we did nothin' the live-long day and all the dark hours of the night but dance and drink, put money on horses and ruin women. Do we never do a stroke of work? Is this the one plague-spot in Holy Ireland?'

'Ah, God help him!' said Jerry with a sad shake of his head. 'If the poor divil only knew. All the trouble in this parish happens on the road home from evenin' devotions.'

And Jerry looked so serious and so comical that the men all laughed until the drink sang in their heads.

Dan Byrne clapped Jerry on the back and asked when he had last been to evening devotions.

'I am in everything the Church's man,' Jerry answered and lifted his pint in salutation.

'You don't mean to tell me, Jerry,' said the Growler, 'that ye're goin' to give in? The Church in this country is getting altogether too graspin'. If we don't resist, they'll be takin' the shirts off our backs next.'

'Growler,' said Jerry. 'Have a care. Think of yer immortal soul, hoverin' on the brink of destruction. What the hell does yer shirt matter? That car is goin' to get its oats.'

Two days later Father Tracy tried in vain to start his car. He took out the plugs and cleaned them, tickled the carburettor, poured kettles of hot water into the radiator. Not a stir. The engine was as dead as mutton. When he had exhausted his small store of mechanical knowledge and his temper, he sent for a mechanic. Someone had poured about a stone of oats into the petrol tank.

There wasn't any doubt, the men agreed, but that Jerry MacAvoy was a great card.

From that day Father Tracy's car seemed to suffer from the world's spite. Not a week passed but something went wrong. Father Tracy learned with fury and amazement all the misfortunes that could happen to a car. Then for a whole week he was kept at home by the disappearance of the battery.

No one knows, even now, after four years, who was the first to lay hands on that battery. Only one fact has emerged and that is that everyone in the village had it at one time or another, in his possession. It had apparently moved from one house to another without human agency and was finally discovered, completely exhausted, by Father Tracy himself, on the steps of the church.

This time Father Tracy acted. The head of each household was summoned to appear at the District Court to answer the charge of purloining Father Tracy's battery. And since Father Tracy was a fanatical Gaelic enthusiast, the summonses were served in both English and Gaelic.

'The English,' said Jerry that night in Delahunty's bar, 'is to show us what we're in for in this world and the Irish is to strike terror into our immortal souls.'

The Growler looked up. He was sitting at the back of the bar, poring over the summons with the help of O'Growney's grammar and Father Dineen's dictionary.

'There are three mistakes in the Irish,' he said triumphantly. 'Three mistakes. What do ye think of that? What are we payin' for?'

'Make a careful note of them, Growler,' said Jerry. 'Be ye sure to point them out to Saint Peter. For very shame, then, he'll maybe let us pass.'

'And but this is no joke,' said Dan Byrne, the shoemaker. 'Here we are, one and all, summonsed. We've got to do somethin'.'

'What I want to know,' said Jim Doyle, 'is how in the Holy Name he got to know the whereabouts of the battery?'

'Abuse of the confessional,' said the Growler. 'The women runnin' to dear Father Tracy wit' their little sins. God forgive them! It's time their wings was clipped.'

'Don't be talkin', Growler,' said Jerry, with some impatience. 'Who in hell would be bothered to confess a battery? Sure it wouldn't be hard to find out all about it seein' it was sittin' open to the public view, in every house in the place.'

'Still and all,' said the Growler, nodding his head, 'This is tyranny and no mistake.'

'Well the way I look at it,' said Delahunty from the other

side of the bar, 'it would be a shockin' scandal if it came to court. Bad for all of us.'

Delahunty was a silent man who rarely mixed in disputes of any kind. Also he was the only one not involved in this affair.

'Bad for all of us, for the village, for business. Best thing to do is to settle the matter right now.'

'We can't stop it,' said the Growler. 'Even so be that we're willing, we still couldn't. Only Father Tracy can do that.'

'Ye never know,' said Delahunty, 'where these things will stop once they begin.'

Jerry MacAvoy put down his glass on the counter.

'Ye're right,' he said. 'I tell ye what. I'll go along to Father Mooney and get him to talk sense into his curate.'

Jerry found the old priest, wrapped up in a blanket and bending miserably over the fire. He was suffering from one of his 'attacks'. On the table beside him sat a tall glass of brandy and water which he sipped almost continuously. From time to time he would place his hand on his stomach and look around in agony. The brandy and nature struggled within him and then up would come the wind in an explosive, resounding belch.

'I'm sorry to see ye like this, Father Mooney,' said Jerry.

The words sounded unpleasantly in Father Mooney's ear. He looked sharply at Jerry. Was the man laughing at him, insinuating maybe that he'd been drinking? It was not a favourable beginning.

'It's onions,' said the parish priest savagely. 'That one puts onions into everything she cooks, knowin' full well they bring on heartburn.'

'Do they now?' said Jerry. 'That's bad.' His mind searched for comfort. 'But they do say that a raw potato'll put things right in next to no time.'

The priest looked wildly at Jerry. His eyes went red with rage. Jerry's face, with its look of comic innocence, infuriated him. The man was sitting there and deliberately making a mock of him, the parish priest, to his face, in his own house.

'Do — you — want — to — kill — me,' he gasped. Again the sudden eruption which stopped further speech.

'Oh, well I suppose it's only talk,' said Jerry. 'Never havin'
been taken that way myself, I don't rightly know.'

Now if Jerry had only been able to produce some harrow-
ing disorder from which he suffered from time to time, all
might have been saved. But to come here, and boast of rude
health, and laugh at a suffering man, was more than flesh and
blood could endure.

'I suppose,' Father Mooney snapped, 'ye're here on some
errand or other. Har'ly to enquire about my health.'

'That's so, Father. It's about this affair of Father Tracy's
battery. Ye see how it is. We don't want the matter to come
up in court. 'Twould look bad for everybody concerned
and nothin' gained either way. Father Tracy's young and
hot-headed and we thought you, havin' the interest of the
village at heart, could maybe head him off.'

Father Mooney glared at Jerry.

'I'll have ye remember, first of all, that it's har'ly your
place to criticize a priest. It's the great vice of this age,
irreverence, lack of proper respect for those set in authority.
Then let me say that Father Tracy has my full approval —
mark ye — full approval. It's time and so it is that this place
learned proper humility and decency. Ye think ye can make
a mock of yer clergy — but mark my words —' Here Father
Mooney was obliged to seize the glass of brandy and water.
He swallowed at least half the contents at a gulp and again
looked around in puzzled anguish.

'Ah but, Father, can't ye see. 'Twas one of the young
chizzlers that done it. You know, one of the young lads,
not knowin' any better.'

'And don't ye see, Jerry MacAvoy, it's your place to
chastise your children; to teach them while they're young
proper respect for authority. Else they'll grow up no better
than their fathers. For thirty years I've wrestled with this
parish, in kindness and patience. Now look at ye — and look
at me.'

'Now, Father, a word from you — '

'I'll not say it, Jerry. I won't say it. I won't hinder Father
Tracy in the course he has taken. Indeed he has my full
encouragement, my full approval.'

Whether it was that Jerry hated going back to the men in

Delahunty's with such an answer, he who was known among them for his persuasive tongue, or whether it was the priest's anger which infected him, or whether he just needed this to turn him against the petty tyranny of everyday life, no one could say. His kind, comical face twisted with anger. He no longer looked funny. He looked downright ugly.

'Is that your last word?' he asked.

'My last word.'

The parish priest leaned back in his chair.

'Well then, hear mine. From now on till the day you're carried feet foremost into it yourself, I'll never set my foot past the door of any church, nor support it in any way, nor give as much as one ha'penny to it or its works.'

'That, Jerry MacAvoy, will be your loss, not God's. And remember that pride is one — of — the — seven — deadly —'

Again Father Mooney's outraged digestive tract seized control. He held his stomach in agony and just as the belch sounded loud and clear, bringing a short relief, Jerry added: 'Sins.'

He took his hat from the table and went out.

Next Sunday there was a notable number of absentees from mass. But the rebellion was short-lived. Pressure from the women, habit and fear drove most of them back. Soon they were all back except the Growler and Jerry MacAvoy.

Janetta's fame began to spread when it became known that Jerry was going to ride her at the point-to-point. Sam Gill, the vet, dropped in on Jerry on his way home from a case and had a look at the mare. Jerry saddled her and led her up to the paddock. Gill watched her as she cleared the sticks, light as a bird. Then Jerry put her at the bank. He pushed her in fairly close before he let her rise. Up she went, changed her feet with the agility of a cat and came down, breathing as easily as a child. Gill passed in under her neck to listen and then shouted his praise.

'You've a winner there, Jerry. But you've got a bit too much condition on her.'

'She's a hunter, not a race-horse. It'll come off.'

'Ah, she's a beauty and no mistake. She'll win the Grand

National yet. Ye'll get a good price for her, Jerry.'

Jerry shook his head.

'No, but I'll win a good few races wit' her. And I'll jump her at the Show.'

He unfastened the girth and lifted the saddle. Standing beside the mare, he stroked her glossy hide, murmuring to her, praising her. Then slowly his strong fingers pressed on the point in her back where the hair divides. She shivered and trembled. A light shudder passed through her limbs. Slowly she turned her head and her dark eyes looked softly at Jerry.

'Hell,' said Gill. 'She's like a woman.'

'Only she doesn't laugh at my mug.' And Jerry's mug looked so wistful and so comical as he spoke, that Sam Gill burst out laughing and laughed all the way home.

One day Father Tracy met the Growler in the street and Father Tracy thought it the time and place to reason with him concerning his absence from mass. The Growler, whose endurance was being sorely tried by his wife's nagging, lost his temper. In beautifully rounded periods, he told Father Tracy what he thought of him, as a man and a priest, what the village thought of him, the townland, the barony, the country, Ireland and the world. He cast aspersions on Father Tracy's truthfulness, honesty and sanity. He insinuated that Father Tracy's female ancestry could not well bear examination and that in the interests of posterity it was a very good thing that he had been priested.

Father Tracy turned pale and trembled with anger.

'Do you realize,' he shouted, 'that you are speaking to a priest of God? Do you realize that I could exercise my power and at this instant turn you into a stone?'

'I don't believe a word of it,' answered the Growler. 'But so be it that ye could, I hope someone would come by and pick me up and throw me at ye.'

The case came up before District Justice Beattie. Even after fifteen years' experience of courts and witnesses, Mr. Beattie could scarcely make head or tail of the matter. There was a flood of half-perjury, at which the Irish are past masters, cross statements, insinuations, scandalous references,

red herrings and irrelevant detail. After listening patiently for
three and a half hours, he dismissed the case and bound the
defendants over to keep the peace. It was, in a way, a victory.

Soon after, the Growler, worn down by his wife's prayers
and nagging, turned up shamefacedly at mass.

When Father Mooney spoke to Anna about Jerry, he got
his answer.

'I have never interfered wit' him, never questioned his
comin's or goin's and I won't begin now. I can only pray
for him.'

And then she said something queer, very queer from a
good religious girl like Anna. 'God,' she said, 'is har'ly the
same as us. He can make allowances, for men are never His
creatures.'

Jerry laughed when Father Mooney took him to task.

'I'll go back, Father,' he said, 'the day they carry you feet
foremost through the church door. Now isn't that a nice
puzzle for ye. By rights ye should die, here and now, to save
my soul.'

It was likely that the idea of the dance was brought forward
by Father Mooney in the first place as a distraction. Jerry's
rebellion was being commented on too generally and, since
he was liked, a certain admiration for the stand he was
making had grown up among the bolder spirits. Father
Mooney, with the help of Mrs. Delahunty, decided to get up
a dance to raise funds for the new parish hall. It was planned
to take place the night of the point-to-point races. Then, if
Jerry's horse won, as seemed more than likely, well you never
knew. God had strange ways of bringing back his own and it
was well known that Jerry had never missed a dance.

Then, the night before the races, the night before the
dance, the Bishop died. Everyone thought that now the dance
would be put off. Not the races, though. Even piety has its
limits.

After long consultation with Father Tracy and then with
Mrs. Delahunty, who had ordered the food and drink, Father
Mooney announced that since the dance was for such a good
object, it would take place. He was sure the Bishop himself

would have insisted. Indeed, it seemed, after due repetition, that the Bishop, on his dying bed, had insisted. What was more likely, as Jerry MacAvoy took care to point out, was that Mrs. Delahunty, a hard, close-fisted woman, had insisted there and then on Father Mooney paying for the food. The drink would, of course, keep.

Jerry sat easily on Janetta's back. But the devil himself was in the mare that day. She cast a nervous, uneasy eye at the crowd which yelled and shouted in the field and an occasional tremor, a light sweating of the flanks, told that she was nervous. Jerry rode through the people, speaking to this one and that, showing off his mare.

She made a bad start. But once under way, she went along quietly and obediently, answering the pressure of his knees, the tone of his voice. She had never moved more lightly, never before gathered her strength together in this way, so that the ground moved under her as if with no effort on her part. She rose, sweetly, to the first fence and then settled down. A point-to-point is run, not with the jockeying of the race-track, but hell-for-leather all the way. Jerry called to her, called her 'his sweet girl, his darlin', his lovely whoore', and it was as if joy and love moved her. She gave every ounce. Three quarters of the way home, she had left the field behind.

Then the sunk ditch, and Jerry did not remember in time. In the very joy of her heart, Janetta rose, cleared the bank and all Jerry's skill could not save her. She came down and rolled over. Jerry had the cunning to roll clear.

When he pulled her up, she stood trembling. Quickly his hands searched for a broken bone, a strained tendon. She seemed alright. The field thundered past. But Jerry forgot the others, forgot the race, on which he had laid far too much money, forgot everything but Janetta. He slung his coat over her back and walked her slowly home.

When he led her into the stable she turned her head and looked at him. Her dark eyes were so full of anguish that he cried out. His hands carressed her tenderly and he found himself shouting, shouting that she must not die, must not leave him. Anna had already sent for Sam Gill.

Gill was cool and business-like. The mare had a twisted gut. A painful accident but not necessarily fatal.

'Ah, don't worry, Jerry. I'll save her. She'll be as right as rain in a week. Ye'll ride her yerself at the Show and I'll be along to see ye. Keep up yer heart, man.'

Jerry, half crazed with misery, kept following Gill about, in and out of the stable, into the kitchen and back again, watching every movement, watching his hands as they touched the mare. And each time that Jerry entered the stable, Janetta turned her eyes towards him and trembled as if beseeching him to free her of this terrible pain.

'For God's sake, man,' said Gill in exasperation, 'Get out of my way. Go to bed. Go and get drunk but get from under my feet.'

Jerry didn't go back to the house. He stood leaning against the stable wall. From there he could see the dance hall, lit up, see the dark forms of the dancers as they passed the windows, hear the shrill tones of the fiddle, the gay shouts of the men. He muttered curses on them, strong, hard curses, spit through his teeth. He swore he would never dance again.

At dawn the dance broke up and Jerry went back to the stable. Gill was standing, wiping the sweat from his forehead with his bare forearm. He was so tired that he could scarcely stand. He turned irritably on Jerry.

'Will ye get out,' he said. 'Ye're no more use than an old woman.'

Jerry paid no heed. He looked at Janetta. The mare's anguished look was like a knife in his heart. He turned away, went into the kitchen and took down his gun. Roughly he pushed Gill aside and shot her. Then, without saying a word, he went back into the house, and throwing his arms across the kitchen table, wept like a child.

That was how Anna found him in the morning.

She would have liked to weep herself. But someone had to attend to the pigs, milk the cow, turn her out to pasture, get the breakfast, attend to the children. It was ill to speak to a man when his heart was sore.

Anna always blamed herself for not being in the shop when Father Mooney came in. Jerry was there cutting up a

side of beef and she had thought it best to leave him alone.
She hurried in when she heard the priest's voice and with
terrified eyes saw Jerry standing there, the chopper in his
hand.

'We thought to see you at the dance last night, Jerry,'
Father Mooney was saying cheerfully, as if there was nothing
but happiness in the world. 'You that's so fond of dancing
and having a good time. It was most enjoyable, I can tell you,
most enjoyable. Still, we missed you.'

Jerry grinned. He had never in all his life looked so
comical, Anna thought, the way his eyes were red from crying, his wide mouth swollen.

'What, Father? ' he said. 'Me go to a dance and the Bishop
dead? '

Anna sighed. Better, far better, for the sake of his
immortal soul, that he had brained the priest.

The Journey Home

Annunziada turned Lap'tite over on the bed, rubbed her back with practised hand and then gave her buttocks a loud kiss. The child wriggled and squealed and kicked. Annunziada picked her up and shouted endearments in a mixture of Corsican French and Provençal.

'Come, little cat, Annunziada will wash you and put on a pretty frock and you'll go a long, long journey to meet your Papa.'

'Pas vrai, pas vrai,' shrieked Lap'tite as she twisted her legs round her nurse's solid waist and dug her fingers into the thick black curls.

'Chaves is below and would like a word with Madame.'

Louise Boyle rose from the tiled floor where she had been lying in a vain attempt to keep cool. She was a small woman with quick, nervous movements. She ran her fingers through her short, black hair which lay dank with sweat on her scalp, and seized a rough towel from a chair to rub herself down.

Then, slipping on a dressing-gown and a pair of mules, and pausing only to light a cigarette, she went down through the dark shuttered house. The heat was horrible. Even though the old house was built for coolness, with high ceilings and tiled floors, and though Annunziada kept the shutters closed all day long, by afternoon it was like a bakehouse.

She found Chaves out on the terrace in the full glare of the sun. He was standing there, tall, lean and still, his brown arms folded over his brown chest, his blue cotton trousers clinging to his legs. His dark grey eyes glittered in their deep sockets against the brown, lantern-jawed face. He had the gentle

melancholy expression of the man who is forever saying farewell to folly.

'Good day, Chaves! Is the car ready?'

'Everything's ready, Madame. But — I've been on the tele-
phone. I think Madame had better wait until tomorrow.'

'What's the matter?'

'All the first and second class compartments are booked
up from Cannes. Not a seat.'

'Then I'll travel third.'

'There is a boat in from Algiers. Madame cannot possibly
travel third. There will be Arabs. They are going north to
work on a new canal.'

'Well, they won't bite me.'

'Their fleas will, Madame. It would be better to wait.
There is the little one.'

Her heart beat thick with panic. Perspiration broke out
anew with prickling intensity. For days she had been full of
an unreasoning fear that in the end something would keep
her back, never to escape again from this cruel sun. She had
come to hate the sun.

'No, no, Chaves. We can't wait. We must leave this
evening.'

'Well, then, I'll come earlier and drive Madame to
Marseilles.'

'To Arles. It saves an hour.'

But in this matter at least, Chaves would not be over-
ruled.'

'I will drive Madame and Lap'tite to Marseilles. There
perhaps we can bribe the guard to put you in a carriage
without Arabs.

'Very good,' she agreed and waited for him to go.

But he did not go. He stood there, in the full heat, looking
out across the stony country over which the Rhone had once
flowed, to a little hill, on the top of which Marius, the
Roman, had built a temple to commemorate some forgotten
victory. There the cypress trees twisted up like black candles
towards the stony sky. There in spring all had been lovely.
There Louise had gone with Lap'tite and Annunziada and
while she had gathered bunches of tulips and Roman
hyacinths, they had industriously searched the ruins for

asparagus and snails. That was before the sun scorched everything but the thin-leaved tamarisk.

'I should have gone north with the swallows,' she said.

Some weeks ago she had stood there on the terrace and watched them. Tired after their long flight, they had rested there on the stony land, tufted still with sparse winter grass. Later, they rose with the sound of tearing cloth and sailed away like a cloud before the south wind.

'Madame is not sorry to go?'

'No, I am even glad. I find the south too hot. I long for green grass and summer rain.'

Chaves shrugged his shoulders and laughed: 'And I, I was three years in the north. I thought I would never see the south again, feel the good sun warm my bones, feel the hard earth under my feet, drink the Rhone wines. I hated the rain, the mud, the cloudy skies, the cold. I shivered. And the women, cold, cruel, money-loving . . . without warmth. And their wine . . . sour vinegar.'

Louise laughed. In every country there is this cleavage between the north and the south, this same complaint.

'Each to his own, Chaves. Yet you married a northern.'

'Because she had red hair. Only think, Madame! Just because she had red hair!'

'She's a beautiful woman.'

'Beauty, Madame, is never quite enough. You should know that. Warmth . . .' His voice trailed away.

Sometimes, when Louise sent Annunziada for him, he would not be at home. He had gone, Jeanne-Marie said, to a bull-fight at Nimes, or on business to Marseilles. She did not know when he would return. Tomorrow, perhaps. Annunziada, in her blunt Corsican way, would solemnly wink one eye when she gave the message but she said nothing. He would come to the villa when he returned and apologize for his absence. It was business, always business. The word, in French, has two meanings, Louise remembered. His voice would be very low, his manners more than usually quiet, his grey eyes more sunken, the lantern jaws leaner.

She watched him as he wandered off with his slow, easy stride through the pine-wood which edged the side of the villa and then returned to the house to finish the packing.

Annunziada had already bathed and dressed Lap'tite and
was squatting in front of her, tying her hair back with a large
blue ribbon. When she had finished, she pushed her own face
forward.

'Une grosse bise, ma chatte,' she shouted. There followed
squeals of delight and loud, smacking kisses. The heat never
had any effect on Annunziada's exuberance.

'Go and lie down, Madame, and I'll see to the trunks. Your
clothes are laid out in the bathroom. Do you really want
these books?'

'Yes, all the books and papers.'

Louise lay down again on the floor. Soon now, soon she
would be off. Soon she would leave this torture behind. But
it was not only the discomfort of the heat which irked her.
For weeks she had been haunted by fear. Sometimes everything around her would assume gigantic size, loom threaten-
ingly over her, pressing in on her. She would dwindle until
she almost touched the earth. Even Annunziada and Chaves
would become monsters from whom she shrank — monsters
of size and brutality. Lap'tite would grow before her very
eyes to twice her normal size. An outstretched hand made
her want to scream in terror. Voices hurt her ears and the
strong smell of sweat and garlic, inseparable from the
southern French, became doubly offensive to her. Then
just as suddenly they would dwindle and she would feel aloof
and distant. Her voice seemed to pass over their heads, and
theirs shrink to whispers. Nothing could come near her. At
that moment she felt that her feet scarcely touched the
ground, that she was living in an unbearable ecstasy. She
could endure it no longer. She was terribly frightened.

It was not until she saw Chaves' car approach the villa that
Annunziada realized that they were going. She immediately
dropped the bag she was carrying, sat down on the floor,
covered her face with her apron and howled. She rocked
back and forward to the rhythm of her wailing while Lap'tite
circled round her with wary curiosity. Chaves came in and
looked at her with the pitying disgust of a superior race.
'Get up, my girl,' he said, 'and carry Lap'tite out to the car.'
For Lap'tite was always carried. Either on Annunziada's
broad back or on Chaves' shoulder. Louise objected that if

she were not allowed to walk, her legs would not grow. But no one paid any attention. As soon as the child was seen heading off in any direction, someone stepped forward and picked her up. She was becoming abominably imperious with all this spoiling. She called everyone, even M. le Cure, 'tu' and swore like a trooper. It was high time, Louise said, that she, too, went home.

There was another orgy of sobbing and kissing when they got to the car. Even Lap'tite's knees were kissed and when Louise turned to say goodbye, Annunziada howled in noisy grief.

'Come back, Madame. Come back to Corsica, to my father's house. There you will live like a queen, without money. We are not like the French. We do not ask for money.'

The Crau lay stony and rough on either side of the road, stretching away to north and south without sign of man or beast until they came to Miramas on its hill. From there groups of sea-pines broke the monotony of the landscape. Isolated farmhouses appeared, then terraced villages and occasional vineyards. Then Mirabeau and the long avenues of trees which lead to Marseilles. Chaves drove well and drove fast, chatting all the time to Lap'tite who sat beside him. Presently she fell asleep, her head against his side. He put out his hand and gently gathered her small body close to him.

He drove through Marseilles at the same headlong rate. Louise clung to the strap in terror. Never before had she been frightened when driving with him. Yet now she was sure he could not possibly avoid an accident. When he drew up at the railway station, her knees were trembling. She sighed heavily with relief when she got out of the car. The first stage of the journey was safely over. Now there only remained to find a seat. Arabs, what were Arabs? Human beings whose skins were just a shade darker than those of the Marseillais. She 'didn't mind Arabs or their vermin. She would have travelled with wild lions.

'If Madame will hold Lap'tite,' said Chaves, 'I'll get the tickets and see to the luggage.' He placed the sleeping child in her arms and disappeared into the throng.

She stood with her back to the platforms and looked

down on Marseilles for the last time. Below her the town dropped steeply away to the Old Port. Beyond, the dark-blue of the many-storied sea . . . From the beginning of man's history this has always been sailor-town. Phoenician, Greek, Roman, Saracen, each in his turn had established himself here and left his blood behind. Every day new sailors surged through the streets, seeking their common relaxations. In sailor-town everything waits for the sailor, the drinking-shop, the gambling-den, the brothel. Down there, at the foot of the oldest streets in the world, they wait. Here girls flower too soon, age too quickly . . .

Someone touched her shoulder. She turned round to find a broad-shouldered, stocky Frenchman standing beside her. He had a round face with light-blue, prominent eyes, fair hair, cropped close, and a sallow skin.

'Let me carry the little girl, Madame. She is heavy. Are you travelling north?'

'Thank you,' said Louise, 'But I am waiting for someone.'

'Ah then, you are not travelling alone?'

'Yes, I am travelling alone. The chauffeur has gone to get my ticket. I am waiting for him.'

'I, too, am travelling north. When I saw you alone with the child I thought I could help. Have you found seats?'

'Not yet.'

'The train will be crowded. You'd better come with me and I'll find a carriage. Come.'

He took Lap'tite from her and led the way. The platform was a milling crowd of Arabs. They pushed and shoved and shouted. The porters stood helplessly by and shouted too. Gens d'armes moved through the crowd with as little effect as porters. They were keeping everyone away from the train until the hysteria died down. Louise held on to her fellow-traveller's sleeve and looked around for Chaves, afraid that he would never find her in this crowd. But he had seen her. Before she realized it, he was beside her, grasping her arm.

'Madame, you cannot go. Come away at once. Those Arabs!'

'I must. This gentleman will find a seat for me in his carriage.'

Chaves shrugged his shoulders and looked at the other with

suspicion.

'I must see,' he said.

They edged their way slowly through the crowd, past the first and second-class carriages, from where the occupants looked on in amusement at the hurly-burly on the platform, secure in their comfort. They came at last to the third class at the front of the train. A porter stood at the door. The Frenchman slid two fingers into his pocket and took out a note. They slipped through. It was as simple as that. Not a word was spoken. He chose a carriage and put Lap'tite down carefully on the seat. She had wakened and looked around with startled blue eyes. Chaves moved to pick her up. The man stopped him.

'I am going to get my valise, friend,' he said familiarly. 'Just stand here in the door and if a single cursed fool of an Arab tries to push his way in, knock him down. I've paid.'

'Here, Madame, are the tickets and the luggage receipts. I've booked through to London. And here is some food Jeanne-Marie sent you. She thought you might be hungry. That Annunziada has no sense.'

'Thank you, my friend, and thank Jeanne-Marie for me. You've both been very kind. And please look after Annunziada. As you say, she has not much sense. Send her back to Corsica.'

Louise was relieved that Chaves did not have to knock anyone down. Her fellow-traveller returned soon with the usual conglomeration of parcels with which the French always seem to travel. They appear to live in terror of starving on journeys. He arranged them carefully on the rack and then took up his place near the door.

'They're calming down outside,' he said. 'They'll soon be piling in.'

'Go, Chaves, please,' said Louise. Don't wait. I'm safe now. And railway stations are about as cheerful as cemeteries.'

'Une grosse bise, Lap'tite, and see you come back soon for another.'

The little girl slipped her arms round his neck and clung to him. 'Come with us, Chaves, come home with us.'

'Poor Jeanne-Marie would be lonely, Lap'tite.'

'Une bise pour Jeanne-Marie,' and she kissed him again.

'You won't be so free with your kisses when you do come back,' chuckled the Frenchman.

Chaves put Lap'tite down and turned to Louise.

'Au revoir, Chaves and again thank you.'

He held her hand. 'A small request, Madame. Would it be too much to send me a telegram when you arrive in London?'

'Of course I will.'

'Au revoir, Madame.' He slipped through the door and was gone.

Just then the porters stepped back and the Arabs came tumbling into the train. The Frenchman took up his place at the door and each time an Arab hesitated, he spoke sharply and the man stumbled on without a word. Soon all the other compartments and the corridors were packed. Now that the Arabs were on the train they became very quiet. They stood leaning against the partitions and squatted in corners, as patient a crowd of poor souls as could be seen anywhere. When the train began to move, the Frenchman came back into the carriage and closed the door.

'Well, that's settled,' he said.

'Still, I feel we have no right . . .' Louise began.

'Madame, we have every right. I have paid.'

This argument, she knew from experience, was final. Money is not the Frenchman's god, but it is his morality.

'Ten years I have spent down there, with those filthy . . .' He checked his outburst and sat down opposite her, broad hands on knees, stout legs a little apart. He looked at her quizzically, as Frenchmen always look at women, measuring her up, placing her, in a kindly way; more an estimation than a judgment. His name, he said, was Jacques Pelletier, and he was native of a small village near Rheims in the Province of Champagne.

'Madame,' he said, addressing her in the excessively respectful third person which Chaves always used, 'Madame is returning to Ireland.'

Louise was astonished. In general the French are almost purposely ignorant of geography, aware only of the countries which press on their borders.

'How did you know?'

'I came into Aldiers one day, on business . . . and perhaps for a little relaxation. I got talking to the captain of a tramp steamer. He had come, he said, from Ireland, from Gallevey. I asked him what the women there were like. He said very slowly, as if he were looking for the words: "The women, you can see the blood under their skin." A sailor's yarn, I thought, until I saw you standing with the child in your arms. Then I remembered.' He put out his hand and touched Lap'tite on the cheek. She stirred gently against her mother's side and smiled at him with drowsy eyes. 'Come,' he said. 'She is getting sleepy. I'll make her comfortable.'

He took down a valise from the rack, unfastened it and produced with the triumphant satisfaction of the professional conjurer, a rug and a small pillow. These he arranged on the seat. Then he took Lap'tite on his knee and removed her sandals with slow clumsy fingers. All the time he prattled to her, clicking his tongue softly against his teeth. Very gently he untied her hair-ribbon, fussing like a hen with one chick. 'So, little rabbit, you will sleep more comfortably. And the beautiful ribbon will be fresh in the morning.'

He tucked her up with exaggerated care under the fold of the rug. Then he sat and looked at her quietly. The heavy eyelids already drooped over the drowsy eyes, the fine fair hair tumbled over her face. Very gently he lifted it, lock by lock, and pushed it back. Then again he touched the soft pink cheek with the tip of his finger. 'She is like a rose,' he said, with heavy sentiment. Then very briskly, he produced a bottle of wine and two glasses from the valise. He pushed a glass into Louise's hand.

'The wine will make me thirsty,' she objected. 'And the water on the train is undrinkable.'

'There is always more wine. Come, let us drink . . . to the journey home.'

Louise raised her glass and tasted. 'A good wine,' she said.

'A good wine, yes. I made it myself. But it can't compare with the wine in my father's cellars. All the world knows the wines of Champagne. But, being Frenchmen, we keep the best for ourselves. When I arrive home, tomorrow evening, my father — he is old now, seventy-two and still mayor of the village — my father will go straight down into the cellars and fetch up the bottle he has been keeping for me. And my mother, who is not much younger, she will go into the kitchen and herself cook the chicken she has been steeping in wine. She will cook it in butter until it drips with goodness and make a salad of crisp, fresh lettuce. Then we'll eat and drink under the lime-tree in the garden. And after dinner the old man will pour some of his best brandy into the coffee and we'll sit there quietly until the nightingale sings. For years I have not dared remember these things. But since my mother wrote to me, I have thought of nothing else. Only think, Madame, tomorrow evening!'

Just at that moment, the door slid open and the ticket collector came in. He examined the tickets back and front with great care. 'One, two, three,' he counted. 'And room for eight.'

M. Pelletier said nothing. Once again his fingers slipped into his pocket and once again a note silently changed hands. The ticket collector saluted and slipped out into the corridor, closing the door carefully behind him. M. Pelletier took up the conversation where it had been interrupted with the persistence of the man who had been silent too long.

'Have you nightingales in Ireland?' he asked.

'Many other birds but no nightingales. Blackbirds and thrushes in abundance.'

'They are good to eat but their song is poor. And they do not sing at night. No, there is nothing so lovely as the song of the nightingale on a summer night, when a man has had a good dinner, when the mind is quiet and at ease.'

'You are going home, then, for good?'

'Yes, Madame, I have sold my farm in Algeria. I have left all that life behind me. My mother wrote that I was needed at home. My brother died last year and my father cannot look after the vineyard alone. So the prodigal returns.'

He poured out another glass of wine and produced a packet of Algerian cigarettes. 'When I was young,' he went on, 'and used to follow my father through the vineyard, I didn't like it much. I was bored and restless. I wanted adventures. Authority was irksome to my nature. I used to look at the posters in the railway station, on the barrack walls in Rheims, pictures of Algeria and French Equatorial

Africa. Pictures of date-palms and yellow sands, of bright
blue skies, of dark-skinned men and women. Particularly
women. Lovely, slender, negro women. The pictures did not
show the dust, the vermin, the heat, the disease, the loneliness. I was burnt up with desire to go there; to leave the
never-ending labour of the fields; to get away from my
father. Well, I have had my bellyful. I have left the best years
of my life down there. As for romance and adventure, I
found little or nothing. I am very well content to return
home and follow my old father through the vineyard. My
mother wrote she has found a wife for me, a neighbour's
daughter. If we like one another, we shall marry. Soon my
sons will follow me. That is how life should go.'

'Even to boredom?'

'Even boredom can be good.' He smiled. 'Though sometimes I think it was boredom killed my poor brother. He did
not seem to want to live, my mother wrote. But, Madame,
too, is going home. That is good. In Ireland there is an old
house and a blackbird singing. A chicken, too, and a bottle
of your black beer. Tell me, Madame, is your black beer as
good as that captain said?'

'It is very good but to tell you the truth it is not so good
as your wine. And our whiskey is good but not so good as
your *Fine de Champagne*.'

'Ah,' he nodded his head with satisfaction. 'Do you know
why our wine is so good, Madame? It is white wine made
from red grape. You have the lightness and sparkle of the
white wine and the bouquet of the red. Like a blond woman
with dark hair — like those Irishwomen the sea-captain
spoke of.' And his prominent eyes expressed the homage
which Frenchmen believe it their duty to render women of
whatever age or complexion. Louise smiled almost in spite
of herself.

'Tell me a little about your life in the colony.'

'There's not much to tell. I worked, I ate, I slept. I rode
over sometimes to spend a night with a neighbour.
Sometimes a neighbour or a travelling official dropped into
my house. We'd have a drink and read all the old papers from
home and talk of the day we could leave. And Arabs, Arabs
everywhere. At first I thought I liked them. They smiled and

were gay and very polite. Then gradually I became uneasy. I found I did not like them so much. You couldn't get away from them. You could do nothing that they did not see. They popped up wherever you went, from beneath your bed, from under the table, from behind a door. You might think there wasn't an Arab in sight when you went outdoors. They were hiding behind trees and watching you. They were sitting in bushes and watching you. You have no privacy at all if you live with the Arabs. They'll only work while you watch them. The moment you look away they stop. So life becomes espionage and counter-espionage. They are lazy, deceitful, verminous, riddled with every known disease and a few unknown ones. Only think, Madame, imagine my horror when I discovered that my cook was a leper . . . . Yet, sometimes, in the evening, when I sat alone, I could hear them laughing and singing their strange songs and telling their endless stories — they are great story-tellers — I envied them. They were not lonely.'

Louise looked at Jacques Pelletier a moment before she replied. He did not look happy, she thought. He looked smug.

'But that is past now. You are going home. For the next thirty-five to forty years, you will rise early, drink your coffee and go out to your vines. You will return at midday to eat and rest and go out to work again. You will marry and rear sons to follow in your footsteps in the old patriarchal way. You will become mayor in your turn. In the summer you will sit under the lime-tree in your garden and listen to the nightingale. In winter you will doze over the newspaper in a warm room or listen to the wind tearing round the house. And sometimes you will walk down to the railway station and look at the posters. And you will never pass the barrack walls at Rheims without looking up at them.'

Jacques Pelletier looked at Louise with something very like anger in his eyes. He shrugged his shoulders and spread out his hands. 'Madame is pleased to be cruel,' he said.

'No. In a few days I shall be sitting in an old Irish house. I shall be sitting in the window, watching summer rain. And that rain, for which I have longed until my soul is sick, will go on for hours, perhaps for days. It gives us the soft green grass which is like a carpet underfoot. It gives us our fair skins through which you can see the blood come and go. But already I shall be feeling the first twinges of rheumatism and remembering the warm sun, its power and radiance. And as time passes I shall long, not for a glass of black beer, but for a glass of the orange-coloured Rhone wine which does not travel and must be drunk where it is made. Nostalgia — an illness of the mind. Place cannot cure it.'

He thought for a moment and then sighed.

'Perhaps, after all, it is just that we are a man and a woman with imagination. Or perhaps all men have still something of the nomad in their natures. Perhaps even those poor devils of Arabs . . . they, too . . .' He reached for the bottle of wine and filled the glasses.

'Madame, another toast, please. To all our journeys!'

Louise looked at the sparkling gold in her glass and slowly raised it. Then she replied 'May the grass never grow under our feet! '

David's Daughter, Tamar
An Ulster Tale

One evening in late July, when the smell of the retting flax lay heavy on all the countryside and the blue Sperrin mountains shimmered in a haze, Tamar Osborne wandered through her father's fields. She came to where a green lane, or loanin', as it is called in Ulster, ran through David Osborne's land, connecting one road with another. She crossed a stile and there in the lane she saw a young man lying, lazily sunning himself. The neck of his shirt was open, showing his broad white chest, and his curly head lay among a bunch of ferns. Tamar was about to pass by, thinking he was sleeping, letting her wild eyes linger softly on his beauty, when the curly head had lifted and a soft, slow voice said:

'Isn't it proud you've grown, Tamar Osborne? '

'Indeed no, John Cloughry, and why for should I be proud? But I thought ye were sleepin'. An' anyway it's a long time since I saw ye last.'

John Cloughry sat up slowly, squinting up at her against the sun.

'Ach, don't I know well, Tamar, that it's just pride. Ye're growin' that lovely now, Tamar, that ye'd hardly speak til a prince, let alone me, though I went til school wi' ye. Ye were a wee cuttie then, an' look at ye now, — ye've got legs on ye like a young filly.'

The colour mounted up Tamar's white neck, reddening her face to the temples.

'Ye've no call, Johnnie Cloughry, til speak til me that way. But I mind that ye were always impudent, — impudent and iggorant.'

'Don't be angry wi' me, Tamar, ach, don't be vexed. Sit down here in the sun and talk a wee while. It's too hot to be trapsin' about. I haven't seen ye this long while, only heard talk of ye. Sit down now and tell me all about yerself.'

'I've no time, John Cloughry,' she said, 'I've a good wheen o' things to get through before the milkin'.'

But she dallied all the same and presently sat down beside him. Gradually the shadows lengthened in the lane yet she paid no heed. She laughed softly, running her fingers through the grass as she listened to his soft voice, cajoling and complimenting her. Then suddenly she felt the cool of the evening, shivered, and looking up, saw that it was now late.

'I must go now. I doubt it's all hours,' she said, 'I'll be late for the milkin' and father'll be vexed.'

'An' I must go too,' he said, 'though I be loathe to; but ould Henderson must be measured for his coffin again nightfall. Come here, Tamar, and give me a kiss.'

'Indeed an' I will not then,' she replied, flushing hotly again.

'An' why not?' he asked, looking at her with laughing eyes. 'Ye're surely not afeart of me, or have ye never given a man a kiss yet?'

'Indeed an' I have not,' she replied with a great show of spirit.

'Well, then, isn't it time ye began? Come, Tamar, dear, give me a kiss.'

And he looked at her so beseechingly, as if she had hurt him in some way, that she stretched forward her long neck and offered him her mouth, very shyly, with downcast eyes.

He threw his arms about her and pressing her closely to him, he kissed her wildly, her eyes, her hair, her beautiful red mouth and her long white neck.

She broke from him and ran towards the stile. But he caught her skirt and held it, and looking at her he cried:

'When are ye comin' til see me again, Tamar?'

'I dunno,' she answered dully, for her tongue felt thick in her mouth.

'Come again, soon. Come the morrow, at nine o'clock. I'll be finished work by then.'

She nodded her head, unable to speak.

When his daughter Tamar was late for the milking, David Osborne grew anxious and his anxiety made him very irritable. He kept walking to and fro, looking towards the orchard, as if she were hidden somewhere among the apple-trees. He called her: 'Tamar, Tamar! ' But there was no answer.

Then he turned angrily towards the servant girl who was waiting with the cans and said gruffly:

'Get on wi' the milkin', Jenny. She'll maybe be back in a wee minit.'

David Osborne was one of the strong farmers of that countryside. He was an honest man, a hard man and a man of God. Austere and just, he robbed no man and let no man rob him. He was proud of his good name, proud of the wealth he had gathered, proud of his flocks and herds and his wide fields. But he was proudest of his only child, his daughter Tamar. He loved her above all his possessions.

Every evening when dusk was falling, he would stand at the front door of his great farmhouse and gaze across the fields, reckoning the yield of this field or that, wondering what price the crops would fetch, looking at his great flax-pits, the largest in all the lands that border on Lough Neagh. Then filled with pride, he would watch his cows being driven from the pastures for the milking and count them as they came, one by one, their heads bent, their udders heavy with milk. Then he would follow them to the byre and watch his daughter Tamar milk, her lovely, young, red head resting against the cow's silken flank and listen to her young voice as she sang some country song while the milk flowed in long regular squirts into the great can between her legs.

She was a lovely girl, David Osborne's daughter Tamar. Though she was not yet sixteen years of age, every young man in the countryside cast longing glances at her as she walked into the Meetinghouse with her father on Sunday, and when on market days she stood by his side as he bought or sold cattle, many a one would say: 'I'll give ye what price ye like for that beast, David Osborne, if ye give me that girl for a luck penny.'

And David Osborne's face would harden; he would straighten his broad shoulders in anger, for he hated the thought of giving his daughter in marriage to any man, or of letting any stranger have a claim on his beloved land.

Every evening when the milking was over and the work in the kitchen ended, Tamar would follow her father into the "room", light the tall lamp in the middle of the table, bring the Word of God from the small table in the window and place it before her father. Then going over to the horsehair sofa that stood against the wall, she would sit there, her hands folded, while he read her long chapters concerning the anger of God against His people Israel, her wild eyes looking quietly at him, her wild thoughts far away.

When she slipped into the kitchen like a shadow, the members of the household were having their evening meal. David Osborne did not speak to her. He arose, as was his custom, when the meal was over and went down the passage to the "room". Tamar followed him, her heart beating thickly in her throat. She lit the lamp and fetched the Bible. Though it was summer it was always dark in the "room", for heavy blinds and curtains covered the window. Then, when she had sat down on the sofa, her father spoke:

'Ye were late for the milkin', daughter.'

'I went for a wee dander through the fields an' I met a neighbour in the loanin', and stopped til talk a wee while.'

'Who did ye meet?'

'John Cloughry, the carpenter.'

'Do ye not know that John Cloughry is a Catholic?'

'Aye, Father, I do so.'

'An' have I not toul' ye, Tamar, that ye should hold no conversation wi' their sort. Ye should min' that ye are one of the congregation of the Lord, one of his elect. I do not say that ye should not pass the time of day as ye go by, but ye must not linger. Bide quietly in yer own house and them that wants til speak til ye can come here. Think shame on yerself, Tamar, that ye should so far forget yerself as til stand talkin' wi' one of his like til the sun had near set.'

Tamar bowed her head, the red colour flooded her cheeks and her heart beat strongly. She did not defend herself in any way. Indeed what would be the use? For David Osborne was not the man to listen to excuses. So Tamar, afraid to meet his angry glance and his frowning brows, hung her head and said, 'Aye, Father'.

Then David Osborne opened the Word of God and read to his daughter of the manifold transgressions of the people of Israel and of God's anger against them. But Tamar's wild thoughts were far away.

The next night, when the Bible reading was over, Tamar went upstairs to her room. She looked at her face in the small mirror over the dressing table and taking up her comb, began to arrange her hair this way and that. She tied it up with one ribbon, then with another. The great clock in the hallway chimed nine.

In her breast, her heart beat rapidly. 'The clock's fast,' she said, half-aloud.

Then she crossed to the window and looked out. There was a sloping roof beneath, covering a shed which stood in the garden. She took off her shoes and stockings and fastened them round her neck. Then, clambering out of the window, she climbed slowly down the roof and dropped onto the ground. She ran quickly through the garden before stopping to put on her shoes and stockings. Then, her heart choking her, she ran through the fields towards the grassy lane.

He seized her as she was crossing the stile and carried her, half-protesting, to the grassy bank.

'Ach, Tamar, Tamar!' he cried, 'I thought ye were never comin'.'

'Why, it's har'ly nine yet!' said Tamar.

'Ach, my dear, I've been here hours and hours lookin' out over the fields for ye, wunnerin' would ye ever come.'

His left hand held her close while his right hand fondled her body.

'Will ye stop, Johnnie Cloughry! Have ye no shame, man dear. Stop, will ye!'

But he did not stop. Putting his mouth close to her ear, he said:

'Tamar, dear Tamar! My lovely Tamar! I love ye. I love ye right well.'

'Stop, Johnnie, stop!'

'Ach, my dear!' he sighed, and let his head fall on her lap, face downward, the offending hand resting on her knee. He did not move, did not utter a sound, and Tamar, looking at him, lost her fear. He seemed so gentle, like a child. She looked at the thick wavy hair that grew on the back of his head, coming down to a little drake's tail on the nape of his neck, and she could not, for the life of her, resist touching it. She ran her fingers through those thick dark curls, feeling their strong growth. Suddenly he sighed and turning round, kissed her hand.

'Tamar,' he said, 'I was that wild the day. I could har'ly do any work at all. I couldn't eat nor think. An' Robert Henderson an' James Watson came intil my shop til see about the coffin an' they stood there talkin'. An' Tamar, they were talkin' about you. They were sayin' how rich yer father was an' how ye would fall in for it all. James Watson said ye were the handsomest girl in seven parishes forbye an' this autumn when the crops were in, he had a min' til go courtin' ye. Ach, Tamar, I could have killed him! I stood there driving nails intil that coffin, wishing I was drivin' them intil his heart.'

Then sitting up, he caught her hands in his and said:

'Tamar, do ye think ye would have me?'

'I dunno, Johnnie. I like ye rightly but I'm o'er young yet.'

'Ye're that lovely, Tamar! No man'll have peace til ye take someone.'

'An' forbye, Johnnie, I doubt my father wouldn't let me.'

'Why wouldn't he? I know I'm not rich like James Watson, but I'm young and strong an' I'll look after ye well.'

'It's not that, Johnnie. It's because ye are a Catholic.'

'Well, if I can forget your religion, surely ye can forget mine. Tamar, it wouldn't matter, dear, if ye loved me.'

'I know, I know. It doesn't matter til me, but still — my father wudna let me.'

'Tamar, say "I love ye".'

Tamar looked at him shyly through her long lashes and whispered close to his ear:

'I love ye, John Cloughry.'

He seized her. She submitted, returning kiss for kiss,

running her fingers lovingly through his thick black hair, no
longer seeking to put away his trembling hands from her
body.

Presently he laid his head again on her lap and said: 'Ach,
my dear, I'm that happy. The morrow I'll go out and get
some good oakwood an' I'll begin til make our bed. An' I'll
put woodcarving on it an' make it lovely for ye. An' when it's
finished we'll get married. I'll go til yer father and say I'm
young and strong, an' if ye don't give me yer daughter, I'll
take her portion or no portion. That'll be a proud day for
me, Tamar Osborne!'

His face glowed with pride, but Tamar's looked dark and
mistrustful.

'My father'll never let me,' she said.

'Surely he will, when he sees yer heart's set on it.'

'No, no. He'd sooner see me dead than married on a
Catholic.'

'He's a hard man and a proud man, they say.'

'He is indeed, an' there's no makin' him change.'

'Aye, my dear, there's one way!'

'There's no way, I tell ye, Johnnie Cloughry, there's no
way. Ye don't know him.'

'There's one way, one sure way, Tamar. If ye loved me . . .'

'An' what's that way?'

'If ye loved me . . .'

'But I do. I do, Johnnie!'

His hands began to fondle her again.

'He's a proud man, Tamar. He's o'er proud of his good
name. He'd let ye marry me if ye were goin' til have a child.'

Tamar cried aloud, pushing his hands from her.

'No, no, John Cloughry, don't do that. Can ye not wait,
man alive, til once we are married? Can ye not wait?'

'I canna bide that long, Tamar . . . . For ye say yersel'
he'll never give way. Do ye not see that, my dear? Do ye not
love me Tamar? Will ye not trust me? My dear, my dear,
ye're more precious til me than the Virgin on the altar!
Tamar, ye're that lovely I'd damn my soul for ye. Tamar,
Tamar . . . dear . . . .'

'I do, I do, Johnnie. I do love ye. But it wudna be right.'

'Tamar, dear love, I love ye, I love ye. There's no other

way, dear girl. An' ye know I love ye, that ye can trust me. Ye're that lovely, I cudna leave ye.'

'It wudna be right,' she kept repeating, but each time she said it, her voice grew fainter and when at last he threw his arms around her, pressing his mouth to hers, uttering little soft noises that were not words, she did not resist.

When she looked at his face again, it was sad, sad and cold and still. He sat there beside her, his head in his hands, his knees drawn up to his chin. She looked at him so lovingly, yearning over him as a mother over her child and wondering why he sat thus away from her, distant and withdrawn. It was now she who made advances. She touched his shoulder quietly with her hand and said softly:

'Johnnie, maybe I'd better be goin'. They might miss me. Give me a kiss, Johnnie, before I go.'

He kissed her, but distantly, as a brother might kiss.

'Goodbye, my dear,' she said.

He got up and went to the stile with her.

'Goodbye, dear Tamar,' he said.

It was now she who pleaded.

'Will ye be here the morrow night?'

'I will so, Tamar.'

'Goodnight, my dear.'

'Goodnight, dear.'

She lingered a moment at the stile, longing for a more intimate farewell. She looked away across the field towards the house and from the pits in the hollow, there gently floated on the night breeze the heavy, sickly smell of the retting flax.

As she crossed the field she looked back to see if, by chance, he were looking after her. But already he was far away.

They met again and again all through the heavy summer months, and when autumn came, she said one day to John Cloughry:

'Johnnie, will ye go til my father now?'

'Are ye sure, Tamar? '

'Sure as sure.'

'I'll go, my dear,' he said and kissed her.

One wet day in late September, David Osborne was driving home from the market in his cart. He sat, bent forward against the rain, a potato bag over his head, another on his knees. The horse, head bent, slowly plodded along the muddy road, across which great pools lay in every dip. In the fields the cornstooks dripped heavy drops onto the stubble, their heads bent over with the weight of moisture. The tall beech trees that lined the road let fall heavy showers mixed with brown leaves when, now and then, the wind shook them lightly. One could not see further than two fields away, so dense was the falling rain. As he turned the corner that led to his own house, a young man stopped him.

'Can I speak til ye, Mr. Osborne? ' he asked.

'Aye,' said David Osborne. 'Speak on. Haven't ye got a mouth on ye.'

'I want til ask ye for yer daughter, Tamar.' he said.

'Go yer road, John Cloughry,' David Osborne replied. 'My daughter's not for one of your sort.'

'We love one another right well,' said the young man.

'She'll over that,' said the father, his voice husky with anger, his eyes glittering under his shaggy brows.

'Aye, maybe,' said the young man bitterly, 'but she won't over what's comin' till her that easy. Ye'd better let me marry her now, an' not have til come askin' me later on.'

'Speak out, ye dog,' roared David Osborne, his voice hard, his face strained. 'What have ye done til my daughter? '

'Ask her yersel', if what I say is a word of a lie. She's goin' til have a child.'

'Ye lie, ye Catholic dog! ' cried David Osborne, as standing up in his cart, he lifted his whip and lashed John Cloughry in the face.

After the cows were milked that evening, Tamar left the servant girl in the dairy to fill the wide, shallow pans on the shelves, and to hand out the milk to the men for the calves. She slipped out past the barns, and ran swiftly through the orchard, her heart beating with terror. She had not seen her father. He had not come to watch the milking, as was his custom. Stumbling over stones, stepping into pools, her head and shoulders drenched with the thick rain, she ran on until she came to the great haystacks in the field beyond the orchard. There she pressed herself into the hay on the sheltered side of the stack to wait for her lover. He was a long time coming. She waited patiently, half-dead with cold fear. The night was falling rapidly, and she could scarcely see before her. She was conscious of strange noises, as if all creation were stirring restlessly. Her wild eyes were more with staring through the dark misty rain. Her thick wet hair lay flat on her forehead and her face was pale and drawn. At last she heard him splashing through the pools of rainwater as he came towards the haystack.

'Johnnie! ' she cried, 'Is it yersel'? '

'Aye,' he replied in a dead, cold voice, 'Is it you, Tamar? ' She ran to him; she clung to him.

'Aye,' said John Cloughry, slowly, 'Ye were right, Tamar, he's hard. Who'd ever think he'd be that hard and bitter! What can I do now? I called on Father Walsh and told him and he said he cudna marry us, not without yer father's consent, let alone a dispensation.'

'He'll never give it, Johnnie. What'll we do? '

'I've got til go away,' said John Cloughry slowly, quietly, looking at his feet.

'Go away? ' cried Tamar, clinging more wildly to him and striving to look into his eyes. 'If ye go, take me wi' ye, take me.'

'After I got home a message came from yer father sayin' that if I did not leave the country, he'd have me arrested, as ye were not sixteen years of age; that he'd give me the chance til clear out. And my mother . . .' here he waved his hand helplessly, 'she was that upset. What could I do? I said I'd go and I'm leavin' for Glesga the night.'

Tamar's hands dropped to her sides and in a strange, amazed voice she cried:

'An' ye're goin' til leave me, John Cloughry? '

He turned towards her, his arms outstretched, his voice

pleading.

'Ach, Tamar, Tamar love, what can I do? If I stay here they'll jail me. I'll work hard there, that hard, dear, and make some money and then ye can come til me and we'll go til America thegither. Tamar, I'll not forget ye, indeed an' I won't, my dear. Be brave, have sense and patience and all will come right. It'll only be for a wee while.'

'An ye wud leave me, John Cloughry! ' she repeated obstinately.

'Only for a wee while, dear. Then it will be alright. Then I'll come back and take ye away. Ye believe me, Tamar, I'll come back.'

'Maybe,' she said, her voice half-dead and cold.

'Ach, Tamar, don't doubt me.' He grew fierce as he protested, 'Don't doubt me, my lovely girl. Who could ever forget ye? Ye'd draw anyone half across the world. I love ye dear, I love ye right well. And I'm comin' back, sure as death. Ye'll be waitin', Tamar? '

'Aye, surely. What else is there for me now? I'll be waitin'.'

And bitter tears were falling down her rain-beaten cheeks.

He began to embrace her, to kiss her wet eyes and cheeks, but she drew back and said,

'I must be goin' now. Goodbye, Johnnie.'

'Ach, my dear, the evenin's early yet. Stay and talk til me. It's our last evening thegither.'

'I must be goin' for maybe my father would miss me. He's maybe watchin' out for me. Goodbye, Johnnie.'

'Goodbye, Tamar dear, dear Tamar. Forgive me. Don't forget me, my dear, my dear! '

When he kissed her pale face, her dark eyes and her soft mouth, she did not respond, but pushing him away from her, she ran sobbing through the orchard. As he turned away, John Cloughry sighed.

As she sat that night on the horsehair sofa, Tamar tried hard to listen to the words her father was reading, but she could not. Her head drooped over her breast and her tear-dimmed eyes gazed down on her cold, wet hands. Her sodden skirt dripped onto the floor. There was a sound as of rushing waters in her ears. From time to time she shivered. From time to time she would raise her eyes and look at her father who sat opposite her, reading slowly and deliberately, as was his custom, following each word with his finger, never raising his voice or lowering it. And as she looked at him, terror would fall on her and her breath would come quick and short.

' "And I, whither shall I cause my shame to go? " ' read David Osborne.

Slowly the bitter tears gathered in Tamar's eyes and flowed down her cheeks. Gradually a sense of her condition was coming to her. She saw the long, weary years stretching before her, long, lonely, hopeless, grey years. She realized some of the suffering which lay before her and knew that henceforth she was an outcast.

Then, when David Osborne had finished reading, he closed the Bible and looking at his daughter from under his heavy brows he said:

'The day, as I was comin' home, Tamar, John Cloughry asked me for ye.'

Tamar looked at her father, her eyes distended, her tear-stained face grey.

'Aye, Father.' she replied, in a low voice, 'An' will ye not let me marry him? '

'Is what he said true then? ' asked her father.

'It's true, Father.'

David Osborne fixed his burning eyes on his daughter, who stood downcast before him, but he did not raise his voice above the usual tone.

'This is a terrible thing ye have done, Tamar, bringing shame on yer father's house. An' yer punishment will be terrible both here and hereafter. The hand of the Lord is heavy against ye. All yer life will be spent in vain regrets and remorse. Through disobedience our first parents fell and were cast forth from their earthly paradise. Have I not said, Tamar, that ye should hold no conversation with a Catholic. The Lord has placed enmity between their seed and our seed. They do not belong to His Congregation. But the desire of the eye, and the lust of the flesh have drawn ye aside from the true path an' yer punishment is grievous.'

Tamar lifted her apron to her face and began to sob.
Through her sobs she pleaded.

'But surely, surely, Father, ye will let me marry now.
Surely, Father, ye will not be that hard. Have mercy, have
mercy.'

David Osborne kept looking at his daughter's slim form
with a steady stare. His face was drawn and white but his
voice was steady.

'When did ye ever hear me go back on my word? I'd rather
see ye die a felon's death than married on a Catholic.'

'Maybe,' she cried, though she knew her words were idle,
'maybe I'll run away wi' him.'

'Ye will not.' he replied, 'For I'd bring ye back and I'd
ruin him. Ye're not yet sixteen years of age.'

'Oh, Father, Father, be kind, be merciful,' she sobbed,
knowing all the while how useless it was to plead, how
bereft of all hope she was.

'I'm a just man, Tamar, an' I obey the voice of God. "Be
ye not equally yoked with unbelievers." '

'Ye'd think, Father,' she cried with passion, 'that he was
a heathen Turk.'

'He is a Roman Catholic, a worshipper of graven images.
But I'll say no more til ye. I've said all when I said that ye
will never be married on John Cloughry. Now go, go an' ask
God's forgiveness, my daughter, for His hand is heavy against
ye. Go now, go.'

Then Tamar, wiping her flowing tears in her apron,
dragged her weary body up the stairs to her bedroom, there
to ponder on her grief and weep all night on her pillow.

But David Osborne stayed below long into the night,
reading the Word of God, following the line with his fore-
finger and muttering the words half aloud. But he cannot
have found comfort there, for, as he read, slow tears ran
down the furrows of his cheeks on to the Bible. He wiped
them away clumsily with his coarse, work-hardened hand.

For he loved his daughter, Tamar, exceedingly.